# THE FIRE TREE
## Book 1
## THE GIRL WHO COULD DISAPPEAR

by **Ken Kirk**

Dedicated to the memory of Pamela Lang,
Cydara Verrier,  Margaret Beatrice Kirk & Cecilia Reynolds.

# CHAPTER 1

"You're not really there, are you?"

There was a long silence, during which the little girl hoped with all her heart that there would be no reply.

"I'm here," the man answered.

The little girl sighed.

"Why will you not leave me alone?"

"Because you are my only hope."

"Your only hope? What do you mean?"

"I mean that only you can help me."

The little girl sighed, again. It was a long, dismal sigh. It was the sigh of a grown woman, well in advance of her few years of life. Cautiously, she looked around to see if there were anybody nearby who could overhear her. They were alone.

"I can hear when you sigh," the man disclosed, his words coming closer to sounding like a complaint than he had intended.

"This is my life," the little girl protested, "And I should be able to live it how I want."

"This is my life, too," he replied, "And I regret that I am a burden to you."

This was the first time that he had ever apologised to her. He had woken her up at night with his loud voice. He had made her jump when he spoke unexpectedly while she was doing her chores. He had made her cry, several times, with his unkind words. She was weary of his unwelcome need for attention.

"I am sorry," said the man, "I have not been myself for the last few days and I regret the way I have spoken to you."

The little girl flinched, taken aback by the kindness, almost gentleness, in his tone. It was something that she had never heard before in all the times he had talked to her.

"I am desperate," he confided.

She thought about the word 'desperate.' She had never heard it before. It was a *grown-up* word, not one that a child could be expected to know. As she thought about it, its meaning came to her, all by itself.

"It means…" he began.

"I know what it means!" she snapped, cutting him off.

She looked around warily, just as she had done when he had first spoken to her, three long days ago. She did not expect to see him and she didn't. He was never anywhere she could see him. He always seemed to be close by, but always out of sight.

"You are young," he said, "I thought that you…"

"How have you not known that I am young?" she demanded.

"I am simply guessing by your voice. You have a young voice."

"You cannot see me?"

"No."

"Are you blind?"

"Yes."

There was a pause as he appeared to think about his reply.

"I am blind," he declared, "But I am not truly blind. I can see, but I cannot see you."

She gritted her teeth and grimaced at the stupidity of his reply.

"You cannot see me," she hissed, suddenly angry, "But why is it that I cannot see you?"

There was a long silence. This man of so many words, who day after day seemed like he could not shut up, was abruptly lost for words.

She looked around and took in the meadow where she was sitting. She began to hear the birds twittering in the trees and the bleating of the sheep. She knew that there was nowhere that he could be hiding, and yet he remained invisible to her.

She stood up and wiped grass seeds from her shabby, tattered clothing, setting her mind to ignoring him and not hearing him. She looked up at the bright sun and it dazzled her.

She screwed up her eyes and wrinkled her nose. He wasn't in the sky, as far as she could tell. She stamped her foot in frustration.

"You're actually in my head!" she said.

"I suppose I am, but only as much as you are in mine."

His words were tinged with a note of sadness.

At that moment, the sound of her father's voice drifted to her ears on the wind. She stiffened. She was very much afraid of her father. She had seen him carrying a scythe, that morning, and he was busy down the hill in the big meadow, cutting grass for the landowner. She cupped both her hands to her ear, like a funnel, and listened intently, but – unable to hear the rhythmic swishing of his blade – she was relieved to realise that she was out of earshot from him.

She clenched her jaw and pushed her tongue against the back of her front teeth to stop it from moving. Then, thinking instead of saying, she put the following words into her mind: *'You can hear me just as well when I think in my head as when I speak?'*

She didn't understand how she could know this, but she instinctively did know it. It was just another one of the many things that she did not understand about herself. It was just another thing that she would have to keep quiet about to her parents, that is if she were to avoid another beating for being *'strange'* and *'not like other children.'* Most seriously of all, and something that chilled her blood to think about it, she must avoid being called a witch. There was only one consequence of such an accusation, she knew, and that was death.

"Yes, I can hear you," the man replied.

"Do you hear all of my thoughts?"

"No, only the ones that you mean for me to hear or…." he said, breaking into the most wonderful, merry chortle, "Or when you forget what you're doing!"

They both laughed.

"I'm just a little girl," she objected.

"You are, most of the time, but sometimes you are not."

"What do you mean?"

There was another silence. This time, rather than endure it, she spoke up.

"I don't like it when you stop talking, like that. For a man who has so much to say, it makes me worried when you go quiet."

"I talk a lot?"

"Yes! You do!"

"How would you describe me?"

"Garrulous!" she grinned.

"Do you see what I mean?"

"No."

"You said *'garrulous'*."

"Yes, I did."

"Does that sound like a word that a little girl like you would use?"

She thought about it and a sense of panic hit her.

"No! It doesn't!" she said, before blurting out a word she had decided to never, ever say: "Am I a witch?"

"No, you're not."

"How can you be sure?"

"There isn't really any such thing as a witch. It's something made up to scare people. It's a name invented by certain kinds of women to scare off people who might want to harm them. When those people hear the word *'witch'* it makes them think twice about their actions."

"I often know what is going to happen before it happens."

"That doesn't make you a witch, either."

"I can hear…." she hesitated, worrying about what she was about to say, "I can hear the… the 'Others'."

"The others?"

"Yes."

"Who are the Others?"

This time, it was her turn to be silent for a while.

"The Fynodderys," she replied, at last.

"Who or what are they?"

"They are the tiny people in the forest. The faerie folk," she explained, surprised that he did not know of them, "I have actually seen them."

"I don't think even that makes you a witch."

"Yes, but the Fynodderys are the good faeries who are kind to people, but it isn't just them that I have seen," she cautioned, "I have also seen the Boggaiynes."

"The Boggaiynes?"

"Yes. They are the bad faeries. They are completely wicked."

The little girl rubbed her shoulder and winced with pain.

"What's wrong?" he asked.

"I hurt," she said, "I hurt from a beating that my father gave me. He beat me for talking about the Boggaiynes."

"I'm sorry to hear that."

"He had beaten me when I had talked about the Fynodderys, a while back, but nowhere near as badly as for talking about the Boggaiynes. He said the Boggaiynes were evil. He said that to even mention them would bring bad luck."

"You talk of faeries that I know nothing about. Where are you?"

"Where am I?"

"Yes."

"You don't know?"

"No."

"I don't understand. How could you not know? You are talking to me. I thought you would be able to tell where I am?"

"Do you know where I am, little girl?"

"No."

"But you are talking to me."

"We talk to each other aloud and we talk to each other in a whisper, all the time without me being able to see you. We talk to each other with your voice inside my head and, still, you are invisible to me. How would I ever know where you are if I cannot see you?"

"I don't understand it, either."

"Are you stood behind me?" she asked, suddenly spinning around, hoping to catch him unawares, "Maybe you are so quick that, no matter how fast I turn, you can stay at my back?

The man rested his head against the damp wall of his prison cell and closed his eyes in concentration, trying to make sense of everything. He had become aware of this little girl three days previously. He had sensed her presence. She was standing in his cell, always in the same corner, watching him. He couldn't properly see her, but he knew that she was there.

"It was you who came to me," he told her.

"No it wasn't!" she admonished, "I was alone and then, all at once, you were with me. You spoke to me, right next to my ear. I was so shocked, I almost leapt out of my feet and left them standing on the floor!"

"You really don't talk like a little girl!" he exclaimed, laughing.

"Nor, often, do I think like a little girl or act like a little girl, either, as far as I can tell."

"How old are you?"

"I don't know. How would I know?" she asked, "I'm a little girl. I can't count."

"You have no idea?"

"I don't have much use for counting. I feed the pigs and the hens, I milk the goats, I gather up all the filth from the floor of the animal sheds, I make a pile of it in the yard and, then, I put down clean rushes across the floor. If I do it well, the owner gives my father enough coins that he doesn't feel the need to beat me. If I don't do it to his satisfaction, my father gets fewer coins and I get a strap or a rod across my hands, my legs or my back and I go to sleep with nothing in my belly."

"I am sorry that your life is not better."

"There may be another beating waiting for me. I am meant to be looking for a stray hen. It is what I was sent to do. Instead," she said, defiantly, "I am sat, here, enjoying the sun. I have looked for that hen everywhere and I haven't found it. That will surely merit a beating. When I have been away too long, my father will search for me and I will hear him calling. When I hear him, I will run up and across into the woods and come out, further down, as if I had been in there all the while."

"Where are you, little girl? Where do you live?" the man asked, tactfully changing the subject, "I, myself, am in Scotland."

She allowed her thoughts to dwell on the word 'Scotland' and it blossomed in her mind, like a flower, and she understood it. She had never questioned where she lived and nobody had ever asked her, so she began to think about it, deliberately concentrating, and the answer seemed to float into her mind.

"I am on an island called Ellan Vannin," she answered, "In a tiny little place called Baldhoon."

She thought about it some more.

"My island is in the sea between Ireland and Scotland. It's half a day's sailing out from England."

"For a little girl who doesn't know her numbers, you know a lot of everything else."

"I don't think I have always been a little girl," she replied, the words coming out of nowhere and leaving her with no idea what was meant by them.

"I am a prisoner," he said, "I am in a prison that looks like a castle."

"And you are in almost complete darkness and there is a smell of smoke and bad water."

"Yes!" he gasped, taken aback by her uncanny accuracy, "You are exactly right!"

"I think I may have dreamed about you."

"Dreamed about me?"

"Yes, but not ordinary dreams, not like the kind of dreams that come on most nights. These dreams are special dreams."

"What kind of dreams are they?"

"They are the kind of dreams…." she began, weighing up what she was about to say and whether he could be trusted to hear it. She decided that he could, "They are dreams that feel real. Dreams of either things that are already or of things that will be."

A few days earlier, the man – Balgair McRory – would, without hesitation, have laughed at such an absurd notion. That was before, several nights in a row, he had begun to feel her presence.

A butterfly, fluttering across the grassy meadow, changed direction and landed on the little girl's nose. She didn't try to brush it away, but lowered herself backwards until her head was resting on the ground. Squinting up at it, she saw the creature start to slowly lower and raise its wings. As she watched, her eyelids seemed to become heavier and heavier. Within moments, she had fallen asleep.

Balgair McRory strained his eyes to peer into the darkness. As he looked, he began to discern the vaguest and most tentative shape of a little girl stood in the corner of his cell. Looking directly at her, he could make out only the most bleary hint of her, but casting his eyes to look either to the left or right of her, he was convinced that he could make out her form in the edge of his vision.

"I am asleep," she told him.

"Deeply asleep?"

"I will be, soon."

He waited and then he gave a little cry as she seemed to emerge out of the air and take form.

"I mean *this* kind of a dream," she said.

"This is…"

"Impossible?"

"Yes!"

"I agree, but I seem to be here and so do you."

"This cannot be real."

"I have long since given up the futility of trying to determine what is and what isn't real!"

The expression on his face told her that the words she had just spoken were absurdly too adult for her.

"You can only be five or six years old!" he gasped, "Perhaps seven at the very most!"

"Yes, true!" she agreed, looking down at herself and sharing his bafflement, "That would, indeed, appear to be the age of this body."

He continued to gawp at her.

"Would you like me to go?" she asked, mischievously.

"No!" he cried, "Please stay!"

She smiled and nodded her agreement.

"You said, earlier, that I am your only hope."

"Yes. You are."

"Your only hope of what?"

"Of escape."

"Why are you in this prison?" asked the little girl, the thought only just occurring to her.

"I was accused of killing somebody."

"It was a crime you did not commit," she said, making it a statement rather than a question.

"Yes. That's correct. How do you know?"

"I know many things."

"How is that possible?"

"I don't know. It is just how it is," she assured him.

Balgair McRory nodded as if he understood.

"And now," she said, "You are going to be hanged."

"Yes, I am. In a few days."

"You told them that you are innocent."

"Yes, but they did not believe me."

"Because your accuser had given money to people to come and tell lies about you."

"Yes."

"Tell me," she asked, slightly distracted, "How is it that I am going to help you escape?"

The man looked at her calmly and with no trace of worry or distraction, "It will happen," he said with the most serene of smiles on his lips.

"It will?"

"Yes. This time it is I who am able to say that I don't know how and that it is just how it is."

She nodded, knowing that he was quoting her own words. She was all too familiar with the feeling he was describing. Suddenly, she jolted as if she had been stung and stood bolt upright. The man looked worried.

"What is it?" he asked, his panic undisguised.

"My father is calling me."

"What will you do?"

"I must wake up."

"How?"

"If I raise my fingers to my eyes," she explained, demonstrating the motion, "And put the tips of my thumbs on my lower lids and the tips of my longest fingers on my upper lids," she said, performing that very action, "And deliberately part them, then they will open in real life and I will…"

She did not finish her sentence, leaving the end of it unspoken, as – in an instant – she vanished completely, disappearing back into thin air from whence she had come.

# CHAPTER 2

Greesha gave a little cry as the brightness of the sun pained her eyes. She took stock of herself and found that she was laid on her back, her face to a brilliant, cloudless sky, and her fingers frozen in the pose of forcing open her eyes.

It had worked! She had brought herself back from her dream. A dream that was real, wherever she had been. How had she known what to do? How, she asked herself, did she ever know what to do? She just knew.

The birds were still singing in the field at the top of the tiny dirt track with the grand name of Brech Woorlach Road. Greesha presumed that they had not stopped while she had been away.

"Greesha!" called her father, clearly becoming angry at her lack of reply, "Greesha! Where are you?"

She sprang to her feet and ran, as fast as her legs would carry her, to the top of the rise, across the ridge and into the woods. There, she dodged and weaved down through the trees until she reached the halfway point. Gathering her courage, she leapt out.

"Greesha!" bellowed her father, "Come here! Come here, this very moment!"

"I'm here!" she shouted, "I'm here! I've been chasing the hen in the woods, but it got away from me!"

"It got away from you?" he growled, rushing to her and sweeping her into the air by one of her arms, "Well *you* won't get away from *me* and your back and your tush won't get away from my strap!"

So saying, he gave her a preliminary blow with the flat of his hand, landing between the backs of her legs and her buttocks.

"Dare to strike her again and I will break your arm!" boomed a very loud voice, filled with fury.

Her father dropped her to the ground and whirled about to face the source of the voice. Greesha sped off and took refuge behind a clump of brambles.

"Who is that?" her father challenged, crouching into a defensive stance.

There was no reply.

"Who is there?" her father called.

No answer.

Her father looked around, turning slowly to cover a full circle, breathing heavily, adrenalin flowing through his veins, and bared his teeth.

"I am the Warrior of the Gods!" the voice roared, now very much closer, "Harm her and I will show you their vengeance!"

Greesha's father quaked. She had never seen him cower before, but he was definitely doing it now. She rolled to the ground, pretending to faint, terrified for what kind of lashing she might receive for witnessing this event, but she kept on listening.

In his cell, in the prison at Keel Bheir in Scotland, Balgair McRory was shaken at his own words. He had known, somehow, that the little girl was about to be beaten by her father. He had been unable to restrain his anger at it. When he had found himself shouting at the top of his lungs, he had been every bit as surprised as the girl's father. It had been like a canon going off. His voice had echoed off the stone walls of the prison and down the stone corridors loud enough to wake the dead. The girl's father had heard it and, now, in the deepest recess of the prison, came the reply of the burly guard who was Balgair's jailor. Cursing and swearing, the jailor stormed towards his cell.

"Warrior of the Gods, is it?" he cried, "I'll give you Warrior of the Gods when I thump you in the throat with my fist!"

The prisoner began to cringe at the verbal onslaught, but then, without warning, he slumped over and started to writhe and moan as sweat poured from his body and soaked his shirt.

The guard's approach was punctuated by a stream of angry obscenities. They ended only when he reached Balgair McRory's cell. Pressing his face against the bars the guard jeered and snarled at the man inside.

"For your sake, I hope you're having a nightmare," he shouted, "Or I will flog you so hard that the stripes my whip will leave on you will make your back look like it's been stitched with red rope!"

Grabbing a tiny, guttering candle from an alcove in the wall, the guard shielded it to prevent the draft from blowing it out. He carried it to a nearby torch and set it ablaze. Waiting until the flames began to take hold, he held it up to the bars. The light from the torch flooded the cell, illuminating the prisoner on a pile of dank straw and wood shavings, arching his back and contorting himself in pain. His shirt was almost entirely black from sweat.

"Lord save us!" beseeched the guard, making the sign of the cross with the tips of his fingers, "It's the sewer fever!"

The jailor considered sending for a priest, but decided against it, reasoning that the prisoner might not have long enough to live to make the priest's journey worthwhile.

Presently, beginning to regain consciousness, Balgair McRory's eyes fluttered. Then he began to blink. The torch lit by the guard had been extinguished, but the door to a box containing a tall, slender candle had been left ajar. The orange and yellow glow from it allowed enough light for the prisoner to survey his soaking wet shirt with dismay.

"I'm sorry about that," whispered the little girl in his ear, "But I had to do something quickly or you might have been beaten to death for your outburst."

Balgair mumbled something semi-coherent to acknowledge her.

"Thank you," she said, "For your intervention. Your shouting at my father prevented a sound beating of my own."

"My intervention?"

"Yes, your intervention."

"For such a young girl, you have a splendid vocabulary!"

Greesha thought, first, about the word *'intervention'* and, then, about the word *'vocabulary.'* Once their meanings had come into her mind, she gave a little laugh as she replied.

"Yes, I suppose I have," she agreed.

"What happened after my shouting?" he enquired in a hushed voice.

"Once my father had recovered himself, he began to drag me back to our croft by my arm. After just a few steps he let go of me, thinking better of it, and gave me a half-hearted push, instead."

"Did he seem afraid?"

"Yes, he did. He was very much afraid."

"Good."

"It isn't every day that a man finds himself being shouted at by a Warrior of the Gods!"

They both started to laugh, but promptly stifled themselves, each fearing being overheard at their respective ends of their conversation.

"You said I should help you escape."

"I did."

"I've been thinking about it."

"You have?"

"Yes. I have had an idea. Well, the beginning of one."

"What is it?"

"When I am awake, I find it very difficult to be anywhere other than where I am. It's not like when I am asleep, when I find it much easier. So, I need to practice transporting myself to another place when I am awake."

"You do?"

"Yes, I need to get much better at doing it when I am wakeful, so that I do not have to rely upon going to sleep to do it."

"That is a good idea."

"Thank you."

"An impeccably good idea."

She clicked her tongue with annoyance.

"I am going to stop listening to your grown up words when you use them!" she scolded, "Because I have to pause, so that I can draw their meaning into my head, and it is…"

She hesitated, searching for the right word.

"Infuriating?" he suggested.

She made a very good approximation of the 'Scottish Noise' – a throaty grumbling sound – to show her displeasure. He found it perturbing, coming from one so young, but made no mention of it.

After pausing to summon the meaning of the word *'infuriating'*, she gave an exasperated sigh.

"Yes. Most definitely infuriating," she declared.

She drew in a long breath and let it out slowly, as a parent might while trying to hold their temper with an unruly child. He smiled at her bizarre maturity, but held his tongue.

"There are dogs at your prison," she said.

"Yes, there are."

"The dogs smell out people who are ill."

He nodded, but then felt awkward, not knowing if she could tell that he was nodding. It appeared that she could, for she continued as if she had taken the nod into account.

"The dogs can smell things that people wouldn't even know were there," she said, "They can tell if people are ill in a very particular way."

He was about to say 'Sewer Fever', but decided against it.

"The dogs smell for Sewer Fever," she told him.

He felt inexplicably irked, having held back the urge to suggest the word. This did not evade her notice. He could tell.

"If one person has Sewer Fever," she explained in a tolerant, patient, very grown up tone, "Then a lot of people can end up dying from it."

"Yes," he agreed, apologetically.

"I have found," she said, with sudden glee, "That if I stare at a hen and concentrate really hard, I can make it run away from me."

He knotted his brows in confusion.

"What I am saying," she explained, being instantly aware of his expression, "Is that if I can do that with a hen, which has only a small head and, therefore, nothing much in it, perhaps, I could do the same thing with a dog."

He made a noise to indicate that he was following her.

"Dogs have much bigger heads than hens, so they must have room inside them for far more contents to do a lot more thinking."

He made the noise again.

"I hope to be able to persuade a dog to do something for me – or, more correctly, for you – if I can concentrate and think at it very strongly."

"Do the hens come back again?"

"Yes, they do," she laughed, "But it is a while before they dare approach me and they look a little timid when they do."

He gave a chuckle.

"You will be kinder to the dogs?"

"Yes, I will. Dogs are good. A dog would rather die than let someone down. They have truly beautiful hearts."

"Which creature has the most beautiful heart?" he asked, thinking – for some strange reason – that she would know."

"Horses," she said, without hesitation.

"Not people?"

"No!" she giggled, "Most definitely *not* people!"

"Have you ever owned a horse?"

The stunned silence that greeted this question made him feel immediately idiotic. What could he possibly have been thinking? He tried to phrase a sufficiently abject apology, but he was not quick enough. Her reply was stinging.

"I could no more hope to own a horse than I could a mansion. I am lucky – and I mean very lucky – if I eat in a morning. I usually only get to eat when the sun is straight above us and, many times, I do not get to eat again for the rest of the day."

"I'm…"

"Yes, I know."

"I'm very…"

"Yes, I know."

"I wouldn't ever…"

"No, you wouldn't."

He opened his mouth to speak, again, but closed it. Words, it seemed, were entirely superfluous.

"I am able to know the sort of man that you are," she said, kindly.

He opened his mouth to reply, but closed it.

She gave another one of her melancholy sighs and, for no reason he could grasp, he sensed that she had a tear in her eye.

"I wish you were my father," she blurted.

He exhaled, sharply, the wind taken out of him.

"I wish you were my daughter."

They both shed a tear and he wasn't the slightest bit embarrassed.

"I won't spy into your past," she said, "I will leave that private."

"Thank you. I am grateful."

"You have endured a lot," she told him.

He took a deep breath and fought to control his emotions.

"Not like you, I haven't."

"That's kind of you to say."

This time, he resisted the urge to open his mouth. She smiled. He could tell that she smiled.

"You only need to think, you know. That is, if you think towards me," she paused, struggling to describe what she meant, "If you think at me, I mean."

"Yes, I know."

"Yes, you do," she said, and they both laughed.

"This is very strange, isn't it?" he suggested.

"Yes, it is, but I think we're both getting better at it."

"Slowly."

"Slowly," she agreed.

"Me, slower than you, little girl."

"I've been doing this kind of thing longer."

"You have?"

"Yes, but I'm not referring to talking to people who aren't there. I mean other things. Different things that get me into trouble. Things that get me…"

"Beaten?"

"Yes."

"Maybe not so much, any more."

"Maybe not at all, from the way my father looks at me. Just so long as he doesn't beat one of my brothers or my sister, instead."

"That, too, might risk angering the gods."

"Really?"

"Oh, I guarantee it!"

They both laughed. He could tell that she was wiping the tears from her eyes. He did the same.

"I want you to know something," she said.

"What is it?"

"I want you to know that how I have suffered, and how I will suffer, is nothing that you could prevent."

"If it were, then I would."

He knew that she was nodding.

"Oh!" she said, as if an idea had just come to her.

"What?"

"I *will* own a horse, one day!"

"You will?"

"Yes, I will. It will be when I ride with the queen with the golden hair."

"When will that be?"

"Hundreds of years from now."

"What!" he cried in astonishment, "How is that possible?"

"All things are possible."

He knew that she was right.

"The queen," she told him, "Will have something in particular that she says."

"What will she say?"

"Let us do this thing!"

He screwed up his face in puzzlement.

"You can't tell if it's me saying it or if I am quoting her," she declared.

"You're right."

"Let us do this thing!" she said, again, this time sounding very grand.

"That time it was definitely a quote!"

They laughed.

"You have a bad habit," she told him.

"Do I?"

"Yes."

"What is my bad habit?"

"I am talking to you in Manx."

"You are?" he exclaimed.

"Manx is my native language, but you…"

"But I?" he encouraged.

"But you speak Scottish Gaelic, for the most part, until you change to English, often mid-sentence."

"Some words are better in English. Some are better in Gaelic."

"I understand."

"How do you know what I'm saying, if I don't speak…."

"Manx," she said, helpfully.

"Manx," he agreed, "If I don't speak in Manx, how do you understand what I am saying?"

"My father understood what you were saying."

"Good Lord! So he did!"

"I think, perhaps, it's that…"

She trailed off into a long silence and he decided not to interrupt her, in either language.

"I think, perhaps," she resumed, "That the act of thinking is a language of its own. Perhaps, whether somebody is speaking or whether they are thinking, the thought inside their head is, in itself, something pure. Something that can be freely understood without translation."

"Wise words for a six year old!"

She snorted. They both knew that she was of no particular age.

"If I can talk to the dog," she advised, "I feel I can convince it to lead you to the tunnel that it uses to go outside when it needs to pass water."

"Will I fit through that tunnel?"

"Yes, you will. I have seen it in my mind."

"You can see the clothing I am wearing?"

"Yes, I can."

"My own clothes were taken away from me, when I was brought here, and I was given these. Can you, maybe, get my cloak and cap, back?"

"Your things are gone."

"Gone?"

"Yes, gone. The jailor sells the belongings of prisoners."

The little girl could sense his indignation, so offered him an explanation.

"The dead have no need of clothing."

He gave an involuntary shudder at her disclosure.

"You could have told me this more gently!" he protested.

"A man has no need of his worldly goods," she said with exaggerated solemnity, "Once he is beyond the realm of worldly cares."

Balgair McRory opened his mouth to tell her that he had been making a jest, but closed it when he heard her giggle. It was plain that she already knew.

"You will have no trouble with clothing once you are free of here," she assured him.

"How will that be?"

"The man in whose name you were brought here will provide you with clothes."

"Who? The king?" he asked, incredulously.

She clicked her tongue in annoyance as if she were enduring the ramblings of an idiot.

"The constable."

"The constable?!!" he exclaimed, in the same tone as before.

She pursed her lips and gave him a stoney look which, even over a distance of one hundred and thirty miles, squarely reached him.

"The constable is a good man and he is one of your people."

"One of my people?"

"Yes. He is one of your people."

"He is Scottish?"

"Yes, he is Scottish," she confirmed, "But he has a whole lot about him that is English."

"I am the same. I was schooled in England. First in Salisbury and, then, in Winchester. Is that what makes him one of my people?"

"No. He is more than that."

"How?"

"He is of the same tribe as you."

"The same tribe?"

He pondered her use of the word for a moment. Then, it hit him.

"You mean Clan, I think, little girl. Am I right?"

"No, I think I mean tribe."

"Tribe? Are you sure?"

"No. Perhaps I *don't* mean tribe. You are not hearing the same word that I am using in Manx."

She closed her eyes and waited for inspiration.

"You and he share the same belief."

"He believes in God?"

"No!" she snapped, evidently frustrated, "I mean yes, he believes in God, but no, *that* isn't what makes him the same as you."

He took a sharp intake of breath, suddenly afraid.

"Little girl," he demanded, "Are you able to know *everything* about me?"

"No. Of course not. That isn't how it works. I would need to behave badly to do that. I would have to be intrusive. I would have to pry. I would never do that."

"The group to which I belong," he told her, "There is danger in it. It could easily cost someone their life if anyone knew of it!"

"The good man is a member of your *order*," she assured him, now completely certain that she had the right word.

"That is impossible!" he exclaimed.

She said nothing.

"Little girl, there could be nobody in authority, here, who is of the same order as I. Anybody who knew of my order would, very likely, want to have me killed!"

Her reply was slow and deliberate with heavy emphasis on every word.

"The good man *is* a member of your order," she insisted, "You and he are members of the *same* order."

He groaned, partly because he had to accept her assurance and partly because he did not want, at any cost, for her to be right.

"My order is an ancient one that dates back eight centuries."

She did not reply, but appeared to be slightly worried.

"My order..." he started to say, but then broke off, picking up on her anxiety, "Wait!" he said, suddenly afraid, again, "When I said or thought *Scotland*, what did you hear?"

She concentrated with all her might, focusing with huge effort on his words.

"I heard you say *Alba*," she said.

"That hasn't been the name of this country for a long, long while."

"How old is the order to which you belong?" she asked.

"My order," he said proudly, "Dates back to the time of the Vikings."

Instead of *Vikings*, she heard the word *Norse*. He sensed it. Simultaneously they both let out a loud groan. They both leaned forward and gripped their heads between their hands. They had both realised the very same thing, at the very same moment.

"You say it, please," she begged, "Say it for both of us."

He said it.

"We have asked each other *where* we are. You know *where* I am. I know *where* you are," he said, "The thing we forgot to ask is not *where* we are, but *when* we are!"

# CHAPTER 3

"I am in the year 1622," said Balgair McRory.

"That is just a number to me," replied Greesha, "Numbers have no more meaning to me than the grunts and squeals of animals."

"What if you were to think about the number?"

There was a pause.

"Oh!" she said, in surprise, having just done as he asked, "That, for me, is a very long time away from now."

"How long?"

There was another pause as she thought, again.

"Around eight hundred years."

"Eight hundred years!" he cried, "When exactly is now, for you, I wonder?"

"I am mostly a child," she mused, "So you will have to let me close my eyes and concentrate."

There was a much longer pause.

"It is the year 793."

Balgair took a sharp intake of breath at this news.

"What is wrong?" she asked, sensing his shock.

"You said that you sometimes know what is going to happen before it happens?"

"Yes."

"Something is going to happen in the year 798. That is not so far in your future."

"Judging from your dismay," she observed, "It is not a good thing that is going to happen."

"No, it is a very, very bad thing. Do not think about it."

It was too late. Greesha had already closed her eyes, pushed her mind five years into the future and opened them. She made a cry of alarm.

"What is it?" asked Balgair.

"Across the next field, there is a dwelling with its thatched roof ablaze. There is screaming and shouting. There is smoke. There are men with golden hair. They are killing people. These are the Norse you spoke about. They are hacking people to pieces. They are enjoying it. They enjoy killing."

"Stop!" Balgair cried.

Greesha jolted back to the present.

"It was horrible!" she sobbed.

"They will invade your island in the year 798. They will be brutal. They will be merciless."

"Wait," said Greesha, closing her eyes.

"What are you doing?" he demanded. "You're not thinking about them, again, are you?"

"No, I am thinking about some of your words. I am making sense of them."

He waited until she resumed speaking.

"If the Vikings are brutal and merciless, as you describe, then my family are in terrible danger."

"Yes, they are. I'm sorry."

"Do not worry," she sighed, "For some things can be prevented and some things cannot. These things will happen whatever I do."

"I'm sorry. I should not have said."

"No, you should. You would have regretted not telling me. I can put this right, for my own self.  I can feel it."

There was a silence and Balgair could sense that she had her fingers pressed against her temples and could hear a noise as if she were straining to do something.

"It is done," she said, "Whatever it was that these Norse did, I have washed it from my head. I no longer know it."

"That is good."

"Am I right in saying that the people in your country who fought the Vikings were something to do with your cult?"

"My order."

"Call it what you will."

"My order – if I pluck up the courage to dare speak its name – is the Brydda."

"The *Brydda*?" she asked, obviously puzzled.

"Yes, the Brydda," he confirmed, "What do you hear when I say their name?"

"I hear the word nuisance!" she laughed.

"Then that is right, for in the language of the Vikings that word means nuisance."

"You fear to call yourself a nuisance?" she smirked.

This time, it was he who laughed.

"Yes, I do fear to call myself that, because my people – who were Picts and Scotti and Gaels – were a nuisance to the Vikings. They would attack them, over and over again, to weaken them and wear them down. They would have few big battles – though there were some – for they preferred, instead, to do their enemy the most harm they could, while risking the smallest loss of their own soldiers."

"I have something to tell you," she said, with a quietness and a sincerity that made him quake.

"What is it?" he asked, filled with trepidation.

She sensed his fear and unease and shared it. When she replied, she spoke in a flat tone, without emotion.

"The time you speak about. The time of your order. The time of the Brydda."

"Yes?"

As if she had conjured it, the wind that had been blustering and buffeting outside the tiny window of Balgair McRory's prison cell, suddenly erupted into a high-pitched moan. It was a sound like a spirit in torment. The dog in the jailor's quarters threw back its head and howled.

As suddenly as it had started, the noise ended.

"Balgair," said the little girl, addressing him for the first time by his name, one he had never told her, "The time you mention – the time when your order began – and my lifetime, here and now, where I exist, are one and the same. The time when the Brydda was born is right now. It is happening as we speak."

There was a clap of thunder and a brilliant flash of lightning outside the window of Balgair's cell, illuminating the whole of its interior for a single second. In the corner, as clearly as if it were daylight, he could see Greesha. She was stood with her hands by her side. There was no mistake and no question about it. His friend across the centuries was no longer a little girl. She was at least twenty years old. A grown woman.

He jumped up and rushed over to her, but she had already disappeared. Through the soles of his bare feet, he could feel that the stone floor where she had just been stood. It was still warm.

"Twenty years old," he said to himself, "How can this be? Twenty years and not a day younger."

He turned as he heard the approaching sound of a dog's nails clacking on the flags beyond his cell. With it came the flickering, dancing light of a lantern that painted the walls yellow and orange. With the animal came the jailor, a short distance behind it.

"He's here. Just a little further," the jailor said to somebody.

The other person grunted.

"He was soaked in sweat," the jailor advised.

"Let me set my eyes on him, then," replied the physician, "For the dog appears not the least bit convinced of his ailment."

"The dog has lost its brain, then, or – at the very least – the use of its damned nose."

A moment later, the two men and the dog were at the bars of his cell. The physician took one glance at the prisoner and looked at the jailor with pitiful disbelief. The beast, who had alerted the jailor to the prisoner's ailment not fifteen minutes earlier, was now competing with him to see which one could look the most baffled.

"This man does not have Sewer Fever!" the medical man announced in a scathing tone, "What in the name of everything holy gave you that idea?"

"The dog!" the jailor cried, "The dog knew he had it! He smelled it on him!"

The dog lowered its head and slank away.

"When the dog came to me," the jailor complained, "I rushed to look for myself and there was no doubt about it. None at all! He was sweating like a pig on a spit!"

"Well, he's not sweating, now."

"I tell you he had the fever!"

"The only one who has a fever around here is you and it's a fever of that lump of wood that sits on top of your shoulders."

The jailor raised both palms to the roof, as if appealing for reason, but quickly let them flop back down, again, as the other man glowered at him. The jailor shrugged his shoulders and shook his head in disbelief, muttering excuses.

"I have better things to do than wander around the tunnels of this stinking pit and listen to your ramblings!" the physician vented.

With this, he strode off, the jailor following along in his wake, still mumbling his grievances.

Balgair McRory struggled upright, propped himself against the wall of his cell and waited for quiet to return. Then, he tried to process what he had happened, only a minute or so earlier.

"I saw her and she was six years old," he said, holding out his left hand, "Then, I saw her and she was twenty years old," he said, holding out his right hand.

He held up his hands, side by side with their assigned ages, and looked back and forth from one to the other.

"Maybe I really *have* had a fever," he pondered, "That could explain why I have been imagining things."

"I prefer the hand where I am six," announced a voice behind him, "Compared to the one where I am old."

Balgair turned and there, grinning at him, was Greesha, back to her younger age.

"Old!" he scoffed, "You regard twenty years of age as old?"

The little girl's grin grew larger, still.

"Ancient!" she enthused.

"I quake to think, then, how broken and worn out you must regard me, at my age!"

"Just remember," she cautioned, "That to a child of five, even someone eleven years of age is an adult!"

"And how old are *you*, now?" he enquired.

"Right this minute, as I speak, I am eight or nine, possibly even ten," she trilled, "Which is a splendid age to be!"

He looked at her, studying her face closely, for a few moments, before pulling back and yelping in surprise.

"I can see you!"

"Yes, you can."

"You were vague and misty, before."

"Just like I said earlier, we're both getting better at this. You are getting better at seeing me and I am getting better at being seen."

They laughed.

"Tell me," he asked, cupping his chin in contemplation, "How is it that I see you at different ages?"

"That is because, I think, that I appear to you during the different stages of my life. Time is not the same for you as it is for me. For you, each minute takes a minute, each hour takes an hour and each day takes a day. For me, I do this – that is, I appear to you – from time to time. I always know what age I am in your terms, and I always know what we have just said to each other. Even so, time is strangely different for me."

"I have never known time, in all my twenty eight years of life from boy to man, to be anything other than it has always been."

"I would have said the same, if it were not for my strange experience of living in my past, my present and my future."

He nodded, despite the fact that her words did not make total sense to him.

"I have discovered," she continued, "That time is not always like a river, where the water flows from one place, upstream, to another place downstream, and where it passes all the points along its way in their proper order. Instead, even though time passes at the same rate for both of us during our conversations, the gaps between them and the order in which they occur, for me, are strangely distorted."

"And this allows you to know what is going to happen before it happens?"

She laughed.

"Yes," she agreed, "I know what is going to happen because I will look back on it – at some point in the future – as something that is in the past."

"How far forward can you go and still continue to see into the past?"

"Until I am thirty."

"Is that when you…"

He stopped, unwilling to say the word he meant.

"When I?" she teased, already knowing the word.

"When you..."

He still didn't want to say it.

"When I die?"

"Yes."

She laughed at him, but not with any malice.

"Tell me," she asked, "If I took off a coat I was wearing and cast it aside, would you hold a funeral for the coat?"

"No. Of course not."

"Then why, when I shed this garment," she asked, gesturing to her body, "Would you mourn it, but you would not mourn the coat?"

"The coat isn't you."

"The coat is as much me as my body is me."

"A coat is just a coat."

"This temporary flesh is no more than a coat we don at birth and cast aside when our use for it is finished."

"When we die."

"When we die!" she guffawed, finding his words hilarious.

Realising that she had offended him, she adopted a more conciliatory tone.

"We don't die," she informed him, gently, "For if we did, it would mean that we had ceased to exist. All we do is simply stop being as we are right now and become something else."

His face betrayed genuine confusion.

"Balgair, you were something before you were alive. You will become that something, again, when your span of living is over."

"I find that very comforting," he said, blatantly meaning not one word of it.

"If sarcasm were a blade," she chuckled, "You could slash a bedsheet into ribbons."

The two howled with laughter. When they had both regained control of themselves, Balgair McRory's voice took on a more sober tone.

"You said that you would have your own horse when you rode with the queen with golden hair."

"I recall saying that."

"I asked you when it would be and you said in hundreds of years."

"Yes, I did."

"How many years will it be?"

She closed her eyes to concentrate before replying.

"Over eight hundred and twenty-nine years."

They both fell silent, neither mistaking the tremendous significance of what she had just said.

"Over eight hundred years," he observed, "Takes you something close to my time."

"No, Balgair. It doesn't simply take me *close* to your time."

He froze and found himself holding his breath. He knew, instinctively, that what she was about to say was something momentous.

"Balgair, the truth is that I am already in your time. I spend a good while, there. I am there often, just fourteen days into what is your future."

With this, she disappeared.

# CHAPTER 4

Balgair McRory was astonished. He sat, with his mouth open wide, gaping like a witless fool. His mind attempted to make sense of what he had heard but, the harder he tried, the less he succeeded.

"I don't understand," he said, at last.

In an instant, she was back.

"It is, very likely, far more complicated than any of us could ever truly understand," she told him, "But, having experienced it, I am starting to see a pattern in the way that things happen."

"A pattern?"

She shrugged her shoulders, "Yes, it is a pattern of sorts."

Balgair continued to look mystified.

"Little girl…" he began.

"My name is Greesha," she said, offering him a smile.

"Greesha," he corrected, "I have a bad feeling that you're not telling me everything. Why do you think that might be?"

"Because I'm not," she replied with disconcerting frankness.

He drew in a breath, preparing himself for bad news.

"The thing I have not mentioned would seem outrageous to you."

"More outrageous than what I have already seen and learned?"

"I will serve my queen with the golden hair both in your time – the time just ahead of where you are now – and in my own time, here, where I am in your past."

"The same queen?"

"The very same queen."

"The same person?"

"Exactly the same person."

"Surely, Greesha, that is completely impossible!"

"It should be."

"It is!"

"Any more impossible than this?" she asked suddenly disappearing and re-appearing before him.

He shook his head in disbelief. She was, now, around six years old, again.

"This, Balgair, is how I will be when I meet her."

"You will be *that* age in eight hundred years' time?"

"I did say that it was outrageous."

Balgair McRory rubbed his forehead, wearily, with the palm of his hand, as if overwhelmed by inexplicable tiredness. She waited, giving him time to gather himself, before speaking again.

"Tell me, Balgair, why have you not mentioned something important to me?"

"I've told you everything!" he insisted, adamantly.

"Have you?"

"Yes."

"You have left nothing out?"

"No!"

She waited for him to change his mind, but he didn't.

"The queen with the golden hair is not unknown to you, is she?"

He jumped as if she had jabbed him with a pin.

"I never thought!" he yelped.

"Really?"

"I seriously never thought! It is as if my mind has been playing tricks on me."

He gripped his head between his hands and looked genuinely appalled.

"She *is* known to me," he gasped, "Of *course* she is known to me. How could she *not* be known to me? She is a hero and an inspiration. Her title – both here right now, as well as for hundreds of years before – is *'Queen of the West'*. She is the queen of Western Scotland in the Highlands."

"What is it that she says?"

He didn't need to think, he knew immediately, and did not hesitate in his reply.

"Let us do this thing!"

"Yes."

"Yet I did not recognise her words when you spoke them to me, earlier."

"Now do you understand, Balgair?"

"Understand? Understand what?"

"That at one moment, you know nothing of her. Then, the next moment, you know all about her."

"It distresses me even to think of it!"

"You need to understand that there is no limit, no restriction and no end to what can happen when it must happen and when it needs to happen."

He was gripped by a feeling of panic, for he did not want to contemplate what he feared she meant, so monumental might be the point she was about to make.

"There will be a time," she declared, "When all the things that are needed will come about and happen."

"The Quickening," he said in a small voice.

"Yes, The Quickening."

"A lot of people say that it is just an inspiring story for foolish people."

"What do you say, Balgair?"

"The Quickening is a wonderful idea, but I have no proof that it is anything more than fanciful thinking."

"Is that what your heart tells you?"

"I dare to hope," he replied.

"But you hold a loyalty and a belief that could get you killed."

"My family, for countless generations have been secret members of the Brydda. It is a tradition passed down from father to son and from mother to daughter."

"In my time, Balgair, in the year 793, who is the queen who rallied her followers to fight back against the Norse invaders?"

"How could I possibly *not* know that?"

"I want to know how *this* time is remembered in *your* time."

"It was Queen Kiffan. She was known as 'Kiffan the Defiant'. That was the name given to her by the Vikings because she would not give in."

"Kiffan did not merely have hope. She believed."

"Yes, she did, but surely her belief was not in 'The Quickening'?"

"She may not have called it 'The Quickening', but she definitely believed in it. She proclaimed that those things that needed to happen would happen and that those people who needed to come together, would all find each other."

Balgair became nostalgic.

"I remember the stories of Kiffan's bravery. They were the earliest stories I ever heard. My mother and my father would tell them to me before I could even understand them. They continued to tell them to me until I did and I had the pleasure of them retelling me the earlier accounts of her that I couldn't quite recall."

"Do you remember the sign she received?"

"Yes," he replied, almost in a whisper.

His thoughts whirled and tumbled, causing him to lapse into silence. She did not speak, not wishing to interrupt him in his reverie. She waited. Once his concentration had returned, he realised that she wanted the answer.

"It was a flame," he replied.

"Yes. It was."

"An exquisitely beautiful flame."

"Yes."

Neither spoke for a long moment, both of them now lost in their thoughts. Neither felt the need to break the silence, because it was a comfortable and relaxed silence between friends.

"You hope, Balgair, but you do not believe," she said, finally.

He looked offended.

"You do not truly believe."

He lowered his head and felt ashamed.

"I need you to believe, Balgair. Alba – or Scotland as you call it – needs you to believe."

He raised his head and saw that Greesha's image had grown absolutely crystal clear. She was, now, more sharply defined and perfectly focused than he had ever seen her.

"Hold up your finger, Balgair," she instructed.

He extended his index finger and looked at it.

"Believe, Balgair McRory, believe," she said, "For these are not children's crib tales you have been told."

He held his finger higher. Instantly a golden haze began to form around the tip of it. The haze gathered itself together, like powdered scratchings of iron leaping to a magnet, and blossomed into the most enchantingly lovely golden flame.

"No!" he sobbed, dropping to his knees.

"Yes," Greesha assured him.

"It cannot be!"

"It is."

"But I am unworthy!"

"In the Paradise beyond this life, Balgair, in the sight of Our Creator, the most meek, the most lowly and the most humble are the ones He raises up to be kings and queens and to be angels."

"I had no chance to bathe or prepare myself before you let this happen," he complained.

"You are cleaner in your filthy skin and your dirty rags than even the most glorious emperor in his silk, his lace and his gold thread."

"This is a dream!" he shouted, "This isn't really happening. I am imagining this!"

"You have never been more awake in your entire life than you are now."

Balgair McRory, staring into the blissful flame, gave a little whimper and a tear rolled down his cheek, but he did not feel ashamed.

She took a step towards him and brought her face close to the flame to admire it. Forming her lips into a circle, she blew gently into the flame. Immediately, the flame grew in height and in brightness.

"Blow into the flame, Balgair."

He blew. The effect was instantaneous and exactly the same.

"The breath of a righteous man," she said.

He looked at the flame, incredulously, and brought it closer to his face.

"Balgair McRory, you have been called," she told him.

He took a deep breath and let it out as a protracted sigh.

"I honestly and sincerely believe," he replied.

# CHAPTER 5

Balgair McRory eventually relaxed his hand and dropped it. He felt a pang of disappointment as the flame extinguished.

"The queen that I know," he recounted, "The one here and now, in this time, is Queen Annis, daughter of Queen Cydara."

"Her mother was murdered," Greesha responded.

"Yes. It was a scandal."

"It was the doing of the men of Clan Campbell."

"Yes, that was the news I heard."

"Have you ever wondered why she trusted the Campbells to be her Honour Guard?" she asked.

"I must confess that, at the time, it certainly did vex me to think of it. The Campbells, after all, are the only clan who are more hated and more reviled than the Clan Grant!"

She raised her eyebrows before replying.

"The new Chief of The Campbells made great play of being contrite and remorseful for the conduct of his forebears," she pointed out.

He rolled his eyes at her adult choice of words and she answered with a contorted, fake smile before continuing.

"In his speeches, when he attended gatherings and events around the Scottish Highlands, he came within a whisker of actually declaring himself to be ashamed of past events. In private, in the ear of several clan chiefs, and most definitely in the ear of the queen, he actually said so outright. Short of putting ashes in his hair and donning sackcloth, he could have done no more to express his sorrow for the Campbells' wicked past."

"His people's shame was short lived," Balgair snorted, "Since they turned upon her and slew her before the year was out."

"The Chief of the Clan Campbell, by making such a public exhibition of seeking Queen Cydara's forgiveness, had put her in a very awkward position. When he offered to assemble an Honour Guard for her from amongst his very best troops, she was almost obliged to accept."

"The glory and splendour of an Honour Guard and the huge prestige that it bestows must present an enormous temptation for any monarch."

"Yes and, this being the case, spurning such a grand gift would have been an almost unthinkable act and would, potentially, have been catastrophic for any chance of building a new era of friendship."

"She should have told him to go to Hell."

"Annis needed to be Queen."

"Annis *wanted* her mother's crown?"

"Absolutely not."

"So her mother *wanted* to die?"

"No."

"Then it doesn't make sense," he replied, making a grumbling noise in frustration.

"Queen Cydara was a beautiful woman, make no mistake about it, but she wasn't merely beautiful on the outside. She was a beautiful person starting from the inside."

"As far as I have heard, everybody who met her said the same."

"Cydara and her daughter may have shared the same looks, the same kind heart and the same courage, but it is important to know that Queen Cydara carefully cultivated and developed a particular edge to Princess Annis."

Balgair raised an eyebrow in question.

"She ensured that her daughter, when required, would be able to be firmer and harsher in her resolve than she, herself, had been. Cydara often confessed that her soft heart had been a burden to her at those times when she needed to be ruthless and cold."

Balgair nodded, knowing exactly what she meant, having had to deal with the very same issue himself.

"There is another thing I should mention," Greesha confided with a twinkle in her eye, "Annis inherited a very particular quality from her mother that flourished and blossomed to a whole new level in her. It was something of which she has remained broadly unaware, but – against some people – it is a potent weapon."

This time, Balgair raised both of his eyebrows in question.

"The weapon I describe is that Queen Annis possesses what can only be described as a feminine allure."

Balgair raised his eyebrows once more, but this time, in appreciation.

"Annis," she purred, "Has a charm and a loveliness that is completely beguiling to most men. She is hardly even conscious of it, but she can capture a man's heart with absolutely no wish or intention to do so. This makes the soldiers who guard and protect her feel not just loyalty, but total and absolute commitment to her. They quite simply adore her."

"She sounds wonderful!"

"You can judge for yourself."

"What?" he snorted, "No! Surely you jest!"

"Not at all."

"I will never meet a queen!"

"You will meet *this* queen."

Balgair shook his head, completely dazed.

"If you do *not* meet her, then all is lost."

"What?"

"As I have told you, Balgair McRory, you are being called. The force that calls you, is not of this world, but beyond this world. Whatever needs to be, will be."

Lost in his thoughts, he stared into the middle distance, not seeing what was in front of him, mulling over the things she had said.

After a while, he turned to her with what sounded almost like an accusation.

"I am disgraced. What would a queen want with a soldier who has lost his honour?"

"You need to go home, Balgair."

"I would not dare, even if I could."

"You must."

"I have brought shame on my family," he insisted, "I have brought shame on my mother, shame on my father and I have inflicted shame and loss of face on my very proud grandmother."

"While you have been gone, the shame has soaked away, like the rain into the soil."

Balgair looked at her sceptically.

"You may give me that look, if you please, but your grandmother will soon be very much elevated in her status, thanks to you, and your parents will almost burst with pride in you."

Ignoring her reply, he continued to press his case.

"My family is of the Clan MacDonald and I have disgraced myself in the eyes of the Clan Chieftain."

"This is all about a horse, isn't it?" she asked.

Balgair nodded, sullenly.

"And you outlawed yourself over it."

"I outlawed myself because I am a horse thief," he grimaced, "I could have ended up being hung for my crime."

"The horse was always yours. It was pledged to you by your grandfather."

"Yes, but in the end, I had no proof of that."

"Not long ago, a document was presented to the Clan Council by the local priest. It was a signed statement clearly indicating that your grandfather wanted the horse to be yours."

For the second time, Balgair's jaw fell open and he gawped.

"You say this truly?" he asked, almost afraid to believe her.

"I do."

"My grandfather died without ever writing a will."

"He wrote a will, Balgair, but the day before your grandfather died, the priest who was given charge of it fell ill with the fever. It was many months before the priest fully recovered. He was close to death on more than one occasion. Only when he had returned from the infirmary at the abbey of Coupar Angus, did the document come to light. You could not have stolen a horse that had been given to you as your own property."

Balgair covered his mouth and his eyes misted over.

"Go home, Balgair. Your father cannot sleep properly since you went away and your mother's heart is breaking. She cries every day."

Balgair opened his arms and Greesha stepped into his embrace. Balgair suddenly jumped in surprise, his eyes wide in amazement.

"I can feel you!" he gasped, "I can touch you!"

He stroked her cheek and touched her chin.

"I am always real," she said, "But sometimes I can become even more real."

"How can this be?"

She contorted her face, as this was something she did not entirely understand, yet.

"From what I can tell, if I spend time in a place and have good reason to be there – having formed a connection, I suppose – then it seems to be that I can very nearly take full physical form."

"Everything that has happened, lately, is strange and unusual," he confessed, "But *this* is far beyond anything I had ever imagined!"

"It is said," she quoted, "That: 'There are more things in this world and the world beyond this world'…"

"Yes!" he interjected, "Far more things, indeed, it appears!"

"You are worthy."

"Thank you," he said, his voice almost breaking.

"I have done nothing."

"You have done more than you could ever guess, Greesha."

"And so have you, Balgair."

"What do you mean?"

"When you fled, you encountered a young woman in distress. She had been set upon by a group of men."

"Yes. It is true, but I only did what any other man would have done."

"The truth is that, in a situation of one man against four, most men would have turned away and ignored her plight."

"I did what was right."

"The Chief of the Clan MacDonald agrees. He feels a debt of gratitude to you."

"Why?"

"That young woman was his daughter, Heather. He feels a debt to you that he can never repay."

"She was The MacDonald's daughter?" he cried.

"She was."

"I had no idea!"

"She knew that. It is why you are far more of a hero than if you had known her identity. Those men would have ransomed her and may possibly have felt it necessary to kill her, if they feared discovery."

"I have gone from horse thief to hero!"

"When you return, you will go from hero to something that you have always dreamed of, as a boy."

"And what is that?" he asked, suspiciously.

"A lieutenant of The MacDonald Cavalry."

"Impossible!"

"Yes, indeed. Isn't everything?"

He looked at her reproachfully for her teasing.

"But, me, a lieutenant!"

"And more, besides, but I won't spoil it for you."

"More besides?"

"Yes."

"What more?"

"Your promotion in rank will be meteoric, to say the least."

His jaw, now well accustomed to the position, obligingly dropped open.

"Surely not!"

"Surely so!" she contradicted.

"I can hardly believe it. It is baffling to think that all these things will happen."

Her reply to him was slow and measured.

"You can be absolutely guaranteed that these things will happen."

"Yes. Of course. I'm sorry."

"I know that they *will* all happen because I can sense a difference between those things that are possible or are only probable and those things that are certain."

Balgair looked sad.

"Knowing my future," he said, "Means that none of these things will come as a surprise to me."

Greesha smirked.

"Oh, don't worry, you *will* be surprised!"

"How so?" he asked, looking puzzled.

"If you were to remember the things I have told you, events in the future might not occur as they should."

"I am hardly likely to forget these things, am I?" he cried.

She threw back her head and laughed.

"Forgetting them will not be a problem for you!"

Balgair contorted his face in confusion.

She waved a hand, dismissively, to indicate that it was nothing that need concern him. Then, walking up to the bars of his cell, she closed her eyes and stood motionless. After a full minute of silence, Balgair could bear it no longer.

"Is there something wrong?" he asked, suddenly worried.

She turned, her eyes still shut, and a long moment elapsed before she opened them and spoke.

"It is time that we got you out of here," she said, as if that were a perfectly good explanation.

She closed her eyes, again, and Balgair waited, patiently, for her to finish whatever it was she was doing.

"The jailor's dog is coming," she said, at last, "And he brings a gift."

The dog in question obediently padded up to the cell door and carefully placed a leather pouch into Greesha's outstretched palm.

"Thank you," she told the creature.

The dog squirmed with joy. Greesha unwound a cord from the neck of the pouch and upturned it over her hand. An iron key fell out.

"This," she announced, handing him the key, "Will get you out of the cell and the dog will show you the route for your escape."

Almost unable to believe what was happening, Balgair reach through a gap in the bars and, after some difficulty, inserted the key into the lock of the cell door. He turned the key and the lock opened. Pushing the door ajar, he looked back to Greesha in amazement.

"Go," she whispered, "Unless, of course, you have grown too fond of your accommodation to wish to leave?"

"You don't need to tell me twice!"

He deftly stepped out of the cell, closed the door and, locking it, handed the key back. Greesha returned it to the pouch, looped the cord back around its neck and held it out to the dog. The dog took it and headed off back the way it had come.

Watching the dog go, Balgair's face dropped.

"He'll be back," Greesha assured.

In a little over a minute, the dog returned, looking thoroughly pleased with itself.

Balgair patted the dog on its head and stroked its coat. He managed to hide most of his disgust as the dog licked his hand, copiously. With a tiny whimper, which could have been either eagerness or anxiety, the dog set off, away from where it had come. Balgair made to follow but, after just a couple of strides, he stopped and spun around.

Just as he did so, Greesha disappeared. Undeterred, he addressed the vacant space.

"Will I see you again?"

There was no reply. His heart sank. Then, she answered.

"In the future. Soon in the future."

# CHAPTER 6

The dog came to a halt next to a round metal grate set into the wall, no more than a hand span off the ground. The dog looked at the grate and then looked at Balgair, expectantly.

"What are you showing me?" Balgair asked.

The dog cocked its head. Balgair looked extremely worried, before breaking into a grin.

"I'm sorry," he told the dog, "For a moment, I thought you were going to reply! Honestly I did, I'm not joking. It's been a really strange day!"

The dog gave a groan, as if it were expressing sympathy.

"I'm looking at a round piece of iron, fixed to the wall," he told the dog.

The dog gave another groan, this time sounding like impatience.

"What?" asked Balgair, as if they were really having a conversation.

The dog reared up onto its back legs and pawed at something further up the wall. Balgair cursed the dismal light offered by a guttering torch, nearby, but – despite screwing up his eyes – he could see nothing. The dog made a noise that sounded like a sigh.

"I'm doing my best!" Balgair protested.

The dog placed its front paws on the wall, again, and stretched up to its fullest reach. Balgair stood next to it and felt with his hand up and down the wall until his fingers found something.

"It's a handle!" he told the dog.

Balgair took a grip of the handle and pulled it. With a dull *clunk* the grate came open. Even in the very sparse light, the dog appeared to be looking triumphant.

Balgair crouched down on his haunches and tried to examine what was in front of him. The light, however, was too meagre for him to make out much of anything. Going back to the dying torch, he pulled out a couple of clumps of straw that had failed to catch light. They were still slightly moist from the oil or grease that served as fuel. Touching the tip of the straw into the flame, Balgair waited until it began to burn and hurried back to the grate in the wall. Depositing his new light source on the ground in front of the iron hatch, he noted that its flames fluttered as a faint breeze took hold of them.

Balgair knelt and lowered his head to the same height as the hatch and peered into it. He found himself looking down some sort of narrow tunnel. Turning to the dog, he made a grumbling noise in his throat.

"I can't believe that you expect me to go down there!" he advised the dog.

The dog, taking this as a dare, climbed into the narrow tube and began to make its way along. The sound of it scrabbling and clambering, as it propelled itself, became quieter and more distant, until it finally stopped. Then, after a minute or so, the noise resumed and grew louder and louder until – before long – the dog's head emerged.

"You are a fine dog and a very intelligent one," Balgair told it, patting and fussing it enthusiastically, "You were showing me how far and how long it is to the other end."

Balgair thrust his head into the tunnel and made a couple of experimental attempts to shuffle forward on his belly. Happy that this was possible, he backed out again.

"The only trouble is, I need somebody to close the grate, after me."

The dog tilted its head to one side and looked at him dolefully. Balgair felt like he was being accused of being stupid.

"Oh! I see. You will do that, will you?"

Balgair could have sworn that the dog winked.

Re-inserting himself into the cramped and worryingly narrow pipe, Balgair began to wriggle his way along it. He had gone only a little way when he heard, from behind him, a gentle metallic click as the grate was firmly closed.

"Thank you," he whispered, "Thank goodness you have big paws."

The dog, he recollected, had seemed to make it through to the outside in around a minute and a half. He was making far less rapid progress, crawling with his arms out in front of him, like a diver might enter the water. No matter how he fumbled, he was unable to gain any real purchase on the walls. In the end, he was compelled to obtain most of his traction by wriggling on his belly like a snake.

After what seemed like an age, he began to smell fresh air wafting towards him. It came in fitful gusts and he could smell the rain. For some reason, the idea of standing in the rain filled him with incredible joy. How often had he complained about getting wet in a shower? How often had he held a cloak over his head, cursing the weather? Many times, he knew! Now, the very idea of getting soaked, in the outside world that lay beyond the prison walls, was intoxicating.

It was night, he could tell, for the light that reached him was measly, at best. When he finally reached the end of the cramped tunnel, he felt like his heart would burst from happiness. He slid out onto his hands and knees, then crawled a little way until he was sure that he was fully out. Then, he slumped to the ground and lay still.

The rain was cool and gentle. It pattered steadily on the back of his raggedy shirt and trousers. It felt good, he decided, to be getting wet from something other than his own sweat.

An owl hooted and he froze. He lifted his head and looked around, scanning up and down the shallow rise. He suspected that the sound was not what it seemed. It came again and he became even more convinced that its source was more likely human.

Whoever it was, they seemed to be waiting, as if expecting a reply. Balgair held his breath. He didn't know what to do. Surely this person could not be waiting for him! That was a completely absurd idea. Nobody could possibly know that he was there. If they did, surely, he would already be dead.

There was a pause, then there came a completely different noise.

"Pssssst!"

This was very distinctly human and done with no attempt of pretence what-so-ever. Balgair knotted his brows and raised his head to look. He began to make out a hunched figure in the distance. It was bent over next to some bushes.

*"Englishman!"* the person hissed.

"He's not English, he's Scottish," said a voice, plainly squat close by them.

There was a grunt of acknowledgement.

"Wait," said the first speaker, after a little thought, "I can hardly go calling 'Scotsman', now, can I? Every head within an hour's ride will turn."

"Use his name."

"I don't know his name! Why would I be calling out 'Englishman' if I knew his bloody name? Did your mother bury your brains under a tree when you were born, instead of your afterbirth?"

There was the sound of a scuffling and muffled curses. Balgair started crawling towards them, hoping to take advantage of their distraction. Before he had covered even half the ground, the two started making snarling noises at each other.

"Will you quieten down over there?" Balgair called, "I'm trying to make an escape."

"There!" said the first one, triumphantly, "I *told* you he was English!"

"Have you taken leave of your senses?" asked the other, "That's not how the English talk, that's Scottish with a wee twang of the English."

"A wee twang?" objected the first man, "I hope I never have a stone in my shoe as wee as that, because there'd be no room in it for my damned foot!"

Balgair was enraged at the volume of their conversation and could not hold his tongue.

"Shut up!" he called, "Do the two of you want us all to be discovered and slain?"

The pair, shocked at his intervention, opened their mouths to protest. Balgair raised his hand, gesturing for them to hush, and hissed at them through his teeth. The two men began to silently mouth foul oaths at each other until Balgair, now only five paces from them, growled loudly.

The man who had run out of insults first, flipped a hand close to the other's nose, almost striking it, to indicate that he was done with arguing.

"We're here to escort you," he announced.

"And risking our lives to do so," added his friend.

"If I only had a sword," grumbled Balgair, "The risk to your lives would immediately double!"

"We're here to take you to himself," replied the first man, either ignoring or failing to process Balgair's threat.

"Then, can you do it a little more quietly, please?" asked Balgair, standing up and approaching them, "And maybe, then, at least one or two people at the prison might remain asleep?"

The two men seemed perturbed.

"We're as quiet as mice," replied the first.

"Even quieter, most of the time," added the second.

Balgair shook his head, wearily, at their absurdity, "Who is this *himself* you mentioned?"

"I couldn't breathe a word of his name!" came the first reply.

"Not even to save our lives!" came the second.

"Is that right?" asked Balgair, as he moved to stand in front of them, drawing himself to his full, imposing height and pushing out his chest.

This time, the men were fully aware of the threat and took a step back.

"He's waiting for you, not far away, in his carriage," one of them offered.

"Is he now? He could be waiting for me at the top of a tree," Balgair told them, "But it would make it no safer for me to trust either one of you."

The pair looked perplexed and distinctly wary, clearly weighing up the wrath they would incur if they returned to 'himself' alone.

"We give you my word... our word... that you can trust us."

Balgair crossed his arms and glowered at them for a moment.

"I will trail you at a distance," he told them, "And I will continue to do so, up to the point where I might begin to doubt you."

The two looked at each other, testing each other's reaction to this offer, and both appeared happy enough, for they began to slowly walk away, pausing only to reassure themselves that he was following. They had gone only ten paces when they halted.

"Wait," said the one in front, "He has sent you some things to wear."

His companion pointed, through the gloom, to what looked like a stunted tree.

"We have hung them on the branches, over by there. They're set on a wee frame to keep them nice."

Balgair could make out some vague, shadowy shapes nearby, swimming in the dark. They appeared to be gently swaying in a light breeze. He eyed them mistrustfully. If he were going to be jumped by some hidden accomplices, he reasoned, then this might be the moment they would choose.

After a few moments of hesitation, he made his way, cautiously, to the spot that had been indicated. There, he found a light wooden construction of half a dozen parallel dowels. From it hung a shirt, a jacket, a cloak, a kilt and, by their laces, a pair of boots.

Checking in all directions, first, Balgair stripped off his dirty rags, using the filthy fabric to wipe himself down, and put on the shirt. It was a good fit. The jacket was an even better fit. Almost a perfect one, in fact. This was despite his tallness and the size of him. He pondered this point, but couldn't decide how suspicious it might be.

He took the kilt off the hanger. It was a good weight and the fabric was of above average quality. He frowned. Even in the dim light, the pattern of it was a little too familiar. He held it up close to his face and tilted it towards the pale radiance of the half-moon. He froze. It wasn't his own, McRory, tartan. It was The MacDonald tartan. A man would only wear the tartan of the Clan to which his own Clan were sworn if they were highly placed. His father was highly placed and so, as his son, was he. This was all too much to be a coincidence.

Balgair paused for a long while, but then decided to continue. He fumbled for the twin belts of the kilt and eventually found them. He buckled the first above his hips. Then, feeding the fabric of the kilt up his belly, he brought it down over the belt at the front. He routed the rest down between his legs and up his back, where he fed it over the rear of the belt. He then wound the rest of it around himself until all the fabric had been used, at which point he splayed it out down to below his knees. He then hoisted the material up to his waist and affixed the second, wider belt, to hold it up. Finally, he skewered the kilt with the long pin that had been provided, to tether the end in place.

Donning the cloak, he suddenly felt warmer. How had he not felt the chill, before? Panic and fear, most likely, he reckoned. With a sigh of resignation, he made his way back to the two men. They were stood in expectant silence.

"This kilt is a MacDonald tartan," said Balgair, accusingly.

They both jumped.

"It's not the wrong one is it?" they both asked, almost at the same time.

"No, but…" he replied, leaving his words to hang in the air.

The two locked eyes with each other and raised their eyebrows, questioningly. A moment later, they shrugged their shoulders and scratched their heads. He gathered they had been following orders and were now unsure if they had got them right.

"It's fine. Let's go if we are going," Balgair urged.

His guides set off, again, heading into the thin mist that was starting to gather. Balgair followed them, several paces behind. They made their way through the sparse forest, mostly keeping to a track. Here and there, the two men held back branches that barred their way. Occasionally they would release them prematurely, causing them to strike each other, sometimes in the face. This would result in arguments and tussles, during which Balgair was sure that he had been forgotten.

After several minutes of walking, during which the two men exchanged the lead several times, jostling each other as they did so, they arrived at the top of a short bank. The incline led down to a broad track, twenty paces below. The two men stood aside, one to the left and one to the right, so that Balgair could approach the brink of the descent, between them.

"We've arrived?" asked Balgair.

"Aye," they confirmed.

In the near distance, Balgair heard the faint snuffling of horses, followed by the stamp of their hooves. He was fairly certain that there were at least two horses responsible for the noise.

"Down there?"
"Aye," they agreed.
"If this is a trap…" said Balgair, menacingly.
"It's not a trap!" they blurted, not waiting for him to finish.
Balgair made the Scottish Noise.

# CHAPTER 7

Balgair reached the bottom of the bank and looked around. Somewhere, in the darkness, he heard the horses shuffling, again, and heard a gentle creak from the shafts of a cart or carriage. He stared and stared into the blackness, but could make out nothing. Suddenly, he felt a jolt of inspiration.

"Falbh!" said Balgair, quite loudly, this being Gaelic for 'go'.

With a jangle of harnesses and a stomp of hooves, a carriage, somewhere close by, began to move forwards.

"Stad!" called a driver to the horses, cancelling Balgair's order.

There was a merry laugh from somebody who, he knew for some bizarre reason, had just put their head out of the carriage window.

"Very clever!" they called, in English.

There was a clattering sound. Balgair recognised it as the shutters being raised on a pair of oil lamps. The lamps were set either side of the carriage, at the front. Twin pools of yellow light promptly reached out to Balgair from what had previously been darkness.

"Will you join me, Sir?" asked the same voice.

"I might do that," shouted Balgair, "And, then again, I might not."

"Are you going to pretend that you have a weapon?" enquired the voice, "A dagger? A sword? A pistol?"

"How do you know if I have a weapon?"

"I can be as certain as I need to be. You have nothing."

"How so?"

"Such things are hard to come by this far from anywhere."

Balgair was momentarily speechless.

"Maybe I stashed a weapon somewhere," he replied.

"I doubt it. If you did, then you would have done well to have been able to find it in the dark. In fact, it would have been damned nigh impossible without a lamp. There has been no sign of such a thing or my men would have seen its light and reported it to me."

Balgair approached the coach, stopping several times on his way. As he neared it, the mist cleared and, above him, so did the few clouds. The moon came out from hiding to enter a broad patch of uninterrupted sky.

The man in the coach noticed Balgair glance around and up at the sky and made an almost conspiratorial comment.

"All that needs to be, will be," he said.

Balgair did not fail to understand that it was a quotation, nor did he fail to comprehend the message it conveyed.

Listening intently, Balgair turned slowly around, looking left and right as he checked carefully along the edge of the treeline.

"I have brought no other to this spot but my driver," the occupant of the coach announced.

There was a scraping sound from within the vehicle as the occupant struck a flint. A moment later, a lantern was lit and hung on a hook in the window. Balgair screwed up his eyes against the glare and lifted a hand to shield them from it.

There came a squeak as the door handle of the carriage began to turn from the inside. In response, the driver leapt down to the ground from his seat. As he landed, Balgair immediately crouched into a defensive position.

"I'm getting the door," explained the driver, reaching for it with exaggerated slowness.

"No need," said the man inside, opening it for himself.

The driver stood back. After a meaningful look from his master, he retired to a good distance, making as if to tend to the horses. In the light of the carriage lamps, Balgair could see the horses were delighted at the driver's attention. As he stroked their heads and tousled their manes, they appreciatively nudged him with their noses and fluttered their lips against him. Balgair noted the interaction and made a mental note that he must be a good person, for he had always found horses to be a fine judge of character.

The door to the carriage opened and the man who emerged kicked down the steps into position with a deft movement. Shunning the third and first steps, he touched his heel lightly on the middle one and dropped to stand on the ground.

Balgair noted that he and the man were of the same height and, surprisingly, with equally broad chests. He was dressed in a fine coat with a brilliant white shirt that had a stiffly starched collar. He wore black trousers – rather than a kilt – and the shiniest pair of riding boots Balgair had ever seen. They had a lustre and a sheen to them that, as a cavalryman, he found was entirely admirable. Noticing where Balgair's gaze had come to rest, the man gave a warm chuckle.

"I insist on taking care of my own boots," he said, leaning a hand against the coach and standing on one leg in order to raise one of the said boots for inspection, "If pride is a sin, then I am truly damned for my love of these boots!"

Balgair found himself laughing along with the man and was a little annoyed to take an instant liking to him.

The man, Balgair decided, was around forty years of age, maybe a little less, and was strong and athletic. His dark hair and dark eyes matched his dark beard, which contained a few random flecks of early greying. He was, without a doubt, a gentleman and an impressive one at that.

"I think we should consider leaving fairly soon," the man advised, "It will be a while before they start to look for you but, none the less, it would be best not to tarry."

"Who?" asked Balgair, "Who will be looking for me?"

The man gave him a weary look and sighed.

"Well, this is not a monastery," he said, pointedly gesturing towards the prison, "So we can rule out it being a band of monks."

"What makes you think I have come from the prison?" Balgair challenged.

"The prison is remote from the city and there are almost no dwellings around here for at least an hour's walk."

Balgair remained silent and only looked at the man, grimly.

"If I meant you harm," the man announced, "I could have shot you with my pistol, fifteen paces from my carriage. It is a very accurate piece of machinery."

"Very well," Balgair conceded, "Maybe – and I mean only maybe – I might have come from the prison."

"You have come from the prison," said the man, emphatically, brooking no argument, "I have good reason to know."

Balgair was about to ask the reason, when his mind abruptly flipped to the man's previous statement.

"How do you know it will be a while before they look for me?"

The man laughed.

"Because I have paid good money for their delay!"

"There is no way you could have known that I was about to escape!" Balgair objected.

"I had an overwhelming feeling about it," the man confided, "I was absolutely certain of it. In fact, in all honesty, I have never felt more certain of anything in all my life."

Balgair pursed his lips and the man looked suddenly sheepish about his statement.

"That," he confessed, "Probably sounds absurd to you, doesn't it?"

Balgair guffawed in response.

"No!" he responded, "It doesn't! Nothing seems in the least bit absurd to me anymore. Not after the things that have happened to me!"

"Strange things. Very strange things. Am I right?"

"Yes, you are."

At this, the man nodded and scratched his head, thoughtfully.

"I knew to come here," he said, "I knew to bring you clothing. I knew what clothing and what size."

The man shook his head, mystified. Balgair could not stop himself from laughing.

"Let me confide in you as my rescuer," he chortled, "If I were to list the strange things that have happened to me, in just the last few hours, you would think me insane!"

"I am relieved to hear it," the man replied, "I am glad to know that it is not only me who is afflicted."

"I can assure you, you're not!"

The man smiled a broad smile.

"Let us leave," he said, motioning to his vehicle.

"And go where?"

"The people and the future of Scotland need you to go home."

"They do?"

"Perhaps you can't feel it, yet, but it won't be long before you do."

"Feel what?"

The man hesitated before replying and, first, gave Balgair a long, steady look of appraisal.

"The Quickening," he said, at last.

"I feel it," Balgair assured him, "I feel it strongly."

The man nodded solemnly, turned and stepped up into the coach. Without hesitation, Balgair climbed aboard after him.

# CHAPTER 8

"I hope you are proud of yourself!" yelled Greesha's father.

"For what? I don't understand," she replied.

"Of course you understand!" he barked, "Do you take me for a fool?"

She shook her head and hoped that she looked as confused as she felt. Silently, she reprimanded herself for having inexplicable insight into almost everything, yet having no clue what her father was meaning.

He stepped right up to her and thrust his face threateningly close to hers.

"Your uncle!"

She blinked in bewilderment.

"My uncle?"

"Yes! Your uncle! My brother!" her father snarled, "That is, my brother who *once was!*"

The words 'once was' registered with her instantaneously.

"Has something happened to my uncle?"

"Has something happened to him?" he gasped, "You know *exactly* what has happened to him!"

"I swear I do not."

Cowering before him, in fear of the blow that must surely come at any moment, she could not stop herself from trembling.

Abruptly the trembling ceased. She found herself standing straight and upright. She fixed him with a steady, even look of reproach. The arm that he had drawn back and held high, ready to unleash violence on her, drew back still further. Her father made several motions to lift it still higher, to increase the severity of the blow, but he never let it swing. There was a look in his eye. He was wary. He was uneasy. He was almost afraid.

"Do it!" she taunted.

Her father bared his teeth, then clenched them, his face a mask of fury.

Greesha wondered where her fear had gone. It had vanished like a wisp of smoke on a breeze. She heard herself speak, almost as a bystander, and was astonished at her brazenness.

"I dare you to strike me!" she said.

Inside, her heart jumped high enough to clear a fence.

*'Have I lost my mind?'* she asked herself.

Her father, almost insane with anger, was gripped with a rage that seemed to completely consume him. He shook as he fought to contain his feelings – his teeth gnashing and his face contorting – but he did not hit her.

Suddenly, Greesha was resentful for all the times he had beaten her in the past. She was resentful, too, for the times he had hit her mother or one of her siblings. She, however, had always been his favourite target.

*'All that needs to be, will be,'* said a voice in her head.

She wondered just how true this might be. She wondered if her father could quell his anger. She wished for it to be so.

Within a second, her father gave a sigh and was perfectly calm. She looked at him curiously, hardly able to believe it.

"You killed my brother," he said, coldly.

He was very definitely annoyed, but he was calm and in full control.

"I can never forgive you for it," he told her.

"I didn't kill him," she insisted.

"You did. I know you did."

He was adamant about it.

"How did I do it?" she demanded.

"You and your damned faery friends."

"I had nothing to do with it and I can't think that they involved themselves, either."

"You made the Boggaiynes sing and, so, they killed him."

She was puzzled. At the very most, she thought, the singing of the Boggaiynes – the bad faeries – would have been a warning. She was certain that it could not have been the cause. Despite this, her father felt completely sure of it and – from long previous experience – she knew that there would be no reasoning with him and no chance of persuading him otherwise.

"You are a dreadful, evil child," he told her, "You are friends with the dark things of the forests and with the wickedness that lives at the bottom of the wells."

She tried to deny it, but he would not listen to her.

"You laid a curse on my poor brother and had the spirit creatures who live in the shadows do the foul deed for you."

She mulled over her father's use of the word 'poor' to describe her uncle. Her uncle had been a short-tempered, unkind man. He had never had time for people in general and, even less time for children, in particular. He had been very cruel to her mother. She had hated him for that and she had hated her father, still more, for allowing it.

That night, Greesha was sent to bed without any food. There was nothing particularly unusual about this, but – that night – it had been done maliciously as a punishment. She was used to having an empty belly and was used to the pain and the cramps that sprang from it. The thing that consoled her was the knowledge that the meagre rations her parents possessed to feed six children, would have gone a little further, that night. Each of them would have had at least a mouthful more food on account of her having nothing.

The following morning, the atmosphere in their tiny croft had been grim. Greesha had heard her mother and father discussing her during the night. Her mother had precious little influence on what happened in their family, but even what paltry sway she held was dismissed out of hand.

As soon as dawn had begun to break, her sister and her four brothers had been sent off to scavenge for nuts and wild berries and whatever vegetables they might be able to find. This left Greesha to endure whatever additional punishment had been assigned her.

Her mother had been in tears and her father had shown her absolutely no concern. Her father had hit her mother several times without even the pretence of a justification. He had also strictly forbidden her from giving her daughter a hug. Greesha had known that it would have been the last hug she would have received from her. How she knew, she could not explain, but had been absolutely convinced.

Her father took Greesha around a dozen neighbours in the hamlets in the near vicinity and made her apologise for being a bad girl and for being the cause of hard times for them all. He also encouraged them to beat her, which most of them had been only too happy to do.

It was she, it transpired, who had been the cause of several animals dying on the smallholdings. This was irrespective of the fact that they had all either died from lack of food or from one of the many possible ailments caused by the disgusting conditions in which they lived.

She was surprised to learn that she was also to blame for the lack of fish in everyone's nets. It was she, apparently, out of sheer spite and mischief, who had caused the nets to catch nothing.

# CHAPTER 9

The walk to the little cove at Laxey had taken the best part of the morning. On the way, Greesha's father had confiscated her shoes and forced her to walk barefoot.

It had not been long before she had cut her big toe on a sharp stone, but her father had refused to stop for her to rest it, even when she had begun to leave blood on the stones where she walked. He had announced, with a callous delight, that he intended to sell her shoes for a copper or two and didn't want her to wear them down any more.

When they arrived at the wooden pier at the mouth of the river, she was hungry, thirsty and hobbling painfully. When she asked why they were there, he told her to shut her mouth and not to ask again.

Her father purchased some food and ale from a man who was selling from a handcart and made her watch as he ate and drank. She went without any kind of sustenance. If he couldn't beat her any more, he had decided, he would make certain to hurt her in other ways.

The sun was high overhead by the time a sailing boat arrived, plying its trade up and around the coast of the island from Peel, Port Erin and Castletown in the South to Doolish, Laxey and Ramsey on its way North.

Her father had engaged in an animated discussion with the captain. This had involved repeatedly gesturing to Greesha and had ended with the captain coming over to squeeze the muscles of her arms and legs and force open her mouth to examine her teeth.

In the end, the captain handed over some coins and her father reluctantly shook his hand. It was clearly not as much as her father had wanted.

"You belong to him now," her father told Greesha, pushing her towards the captain, "He bought you. He owns you."

Greesha stood terrified, staring down at the ground. The captain grabbed her roughly by the arm, dragged her to the side of the pier where his vessel was tied up, and threw her onto the deck. She landed in a heap and scrabbled to her knees.

A member of the crew took hold of her wrist and pushed her down some steps that led below deck. She somehow managed not to fall, narrowly avoiding further injury.

Another person pushed her in her back to propel her into what turned out to be a tiny kitchen. There, she was put to work peeling and scrubbing vegetables. She had never seen so many vegetables. Her stomach rumbled and gurgled at the sight of them, but she thought better of daring to eat any.

A kindly man with a very large, gleaming gold ring on his finger and a silk scarf around his head, appeared in the doorway. He sat her on a stool. Producing an apple, a pear and a handful of gooseberries, he handed them to her. She received them eagerly in cupped hands. Pointing to his own mouth, the man made an exaggerated chewing motion and then patted his belly. Understanding this play acting to mean that she should eat, she tucked into the fruit, eagerly.

When she had finished, the man produced an even greater amount of food and she devoured it with the same enthusiasm. When she had swallowed the last morsel, he hurried off.

Before long, he returned with a tall stone beaker of what she feared was dirty water, but soon discovered to be some form of very weak ale. She gulped it down and he laughed.

Taking the beaker from her, he went away again, and returned with it full to the brim. She very quickly emptied it and he laughed even louder. He went to refill it and – this time – she made sure not to drink it all. She had made up her mind not to seem ungrateful.

The man stopped and cocked his head, listening with rapt concentration to something she could not discern. He lifted his finger for her silence and she obliged. After a few moments, there was a tilt and a sway and the boat drifted away from the tiny jetty. She felt it start to turn, then – as if being urged on, by an invisible hand – the sails filled with wind and it lurched forward, heading towards the open sea.

She felt that she should have had a sense of loss. She'd been thrown out of her family. She'd been sold like a goat or a chicken. She was being taken away from her beloved island. Instead, she felt a wave of relief. There had been a gathering sense of doom inside her and that was now dispelled.

Greesha knew that, had she stayed, it would have been only a matter of time before the first accusation of witchcraft had emerged. That would have led to an inevitable consequence: Death. Not just death, she knew, but death by burning. A death where she would have been tied to a wooden post, a pile of wood stacked around it and then set alight.

Greesha felt herself quake. Being burned alive was a terrible end. She had seen it. She had peeked through a gap in a fence to see it being done, when she should have been at home, asleep. She had crept out and taken up position at the corner of the big field and watched as a hapless old woman, witless and confused, had been burned as a witch.

Greesha blotted out the memory of the woman's shrill screams of torment. They had risen to an almost impossible peak. At the end, it had been like the shriek of a bird. That was a recollection, she decided, that was best well and truly forgotten.

"What are you thinking?" asked the man with the gold ring, in perfect English.

She turned in surprise, her head whipping around to face him. She had no inkling that he spoke English. Especially, not so well. The man had spoken a little bit of broken Manx – her own native language – but had, by no means, been a master of it. His grasp of English, however, took her aback.

She froze. Her mind began to swim. Her thoughts careered around inside her brain like a dozen scalded cats. She didn't speak English, herself! Neither of them could have been speaking English! The man addressed her, again.

"I am not surprised that you don't understand me," he told her, "For Arabic is probably not spoken anywhere less than a week's journey from here."

"I understand you," she said.

This time, it was he who was taken by surprise.

"You speak Arabic!" he cried.

"No, I don't speak Arabic," she replied, "But I can make myself understood."

He looked at her in amazement.

"You are speaking Arabic!" he said, completely baffled.

"No, it is Arabic that you are *hearing*," she corrected.

"You are a jinn!" he gasped, taking a step back.

"No, I am not a jinn," she insisted, very firmly, knowing him to be accusing her of being a spirit.

"Then how is this possible?" he demanded.

She shrugged her shoulders.

"It is possible," she told him, "Because there are more things in this world, and in the world beyond this world, than we could ever begin to imagine."

"If I spoke of this to others, you would be tied into a sack, thrown over the side of this boat and drowned in the sea."

"If that were going to happen," she assured him, "I would not be here."

"What do you mean?"

"The whole of life is like a gigantic clock," she explained, "Every little wheel and cog has a job that it does. Every job that is done plays its part in making the hands of the clock move on its face, at exactly the right speed, to show the time."

"How old are you?"

"I don't know. Maybe I am five and almost six or, maybe, I am six and almost seven, but I am around that age."

"You do not sound to me like a little girl of five or six or seven."

"I wish that I *felt* like a little girl of five or six or seven. Life would be far easier and far less challenging."

# CHAPTER 10

By the time Greesha woke, the boat was unsuccessfully trying to flee a very large storm. The winds had grown so strong that the sailors had been obliged to take down the sails. The rough seas were starting to lift the boat over ever larger waves, flooding the deck with water and drenching the crew. The crew were becoming ever more anxious and agitated.

Greesha made her way out onto the deck, where the man she had seen earlier was struggling to control a long arm that was attached to the rudder of the boat. He and another man were attempting to lash it in place with rope, but they were making very little progress. Every time they seemed to have it under control, it would break free again and knock one or the other of them off their feet.

The man, on seeing her, called to warn her that she was in danger. He motioned for her to go back below deck. She shook her head. She knew that she was meant to be there.

Unlike everyone else aboard the vessel, she was steady on her feet and had no trouble staying upright. This was despite the incessant rolling and pitching of the boat. Slowly and purposefully, she walked across to the man. He watched her approach with a curious look on his face.

"We are going to sink," he confided, "I am sorry to have taken you away with us, only for you to die so soon."

"Nobody is going to die," she replied.

"Little girl, this storm is only just beginning. I have sailed the sea for many years and I can tell you that this is nothing compared to what is going to happen. The waves will soon be as tall as the trees. It will not be long before we are submerged."

Greesha moved to the centre of the deck and stood with her feet apart and her arms outstretched.

"Dear God," she shouted over the wind, "Please spare these good men your wrath and let the sea be calm."

She had no idea why she was so irresistibly drawn to say those particular words, but they jumped into her mind and, so, she said them.

The sailors, all clinging onto the rails to stop themselves from being dragged over the side into the sea, looked at her pityingly, as if she might be insane.

Ten seconds later, the violent winds dropped to a breeze, the heavy seas completely calmed to the very slightest swell and the dark storm clouds suddenly dispersed. The sailors looked at her in awe.

"How did you do that?" asked the man.

"I didn't. I just said some words and it happened."

He looked confused.

"Your words *made* it happen."

"No. The words were of no importance."

The man shook his head.

"You spoke and it happened," he said, stubbornly.

"If I dip a spoon into a pot that is sat on a fire, a pot that is at the point of boiling, then it is not my spoon that makes it boil."

"The pot," said the man, motioning to the sea, "Was just about to boil over and kill us all. The next moment, it didn't."

She thought about this for a while and, then, she knew the answer.

"It is about nothing more than creating the moment. I gave the power that could act, a moment. The power isn't me. The power isn't mine."

This time, the man contemplated her answer.

"It is magic," he said, with a wave of his arm.

The discussion was over, she realised, and – like a child deferring to an adult – she let the matter rest.

"I have a member of my crew," the man said, "Whose stomach troubles him. It troubles him very much. It would be good for me and it would be good for the trade that I conduct, if – by the time we reach Ramsey – he could be healed."

With a certainty that she did not understand, she gave him her answer.

"The healing that you wish for has just happened."

She decided that resigning herself to her strange situation was her best option. Trying to work out the why and the how of everything would get her nowhere. If some kind of mystical force wished to apply itself through her, she reasoned, then she had best just let it happen.

The man hurried away to seek out the one with the troublesome stomach and returned, after a couple of minutes, beaming and smiling all over his face.

"He is well, again!" he announced.

"These acts sap my strength," she told him, truthfully, "It makes me tired. When these things happen, the power that passes through me draws upon me and makes me weak. It is not something that can be done endlessly."

The man nodded, sympathetically.

"I understand," he said, "You must rest."

He did, indeed, understand. She could tell. He would not ask her to perform like some acrobat or juggler. He would not assail her with endless demands.

He had just begun to walk off to tend to some other business when he stopped and turned around.

"I am Asif," he announced, "I am what you might call the 'First Officer' to the Captain."

Greesha performed a curtsey, which seemed to amuse him. In return, he made an elaborate and stiffly formal bow. She smiled and he appeared pleased that she had recognised his attempt at humour.

"You will not sit on a ledge or on the floor," Asif told her, "I will make sure that you have somewhere that is more suitable for a Healer."

When she got back down to the kitchen, she was hurriedly directed away to her own little cabin. It had a bed slung from ropes, just below the beams of the roof, a table, a chair and a padded bench.

Once installed into her new accommodation, she was treated to a lavish meal. She ate everything from a big, gleaming metal plate and, then, the cook demanded that she had second helpings of everything. At his encouragement – no, his insistence – she ate and drank until she was full. She had never had a full stomach in her life. She hadn't even known that it was possible to be full.

Presently, another crew member appeared and emptied a huge shovel of hot cinders into a metal box that stood on legs and was chained into the corner of her room. Before long, the room was wonderfully warm. She couldn't remember the last time that she had been so warm.

With some difficulty, she climbed a rickety ladder up to her bed. There were clean sheets, a woolly blanket and a pillow filled with finely chopped hay and wood shavings.

She felt like she was in a palace. To her, the tiny, cramped room was, indeed, a palace. She fell asleep with a smile on her face, hugging the pillow and, unintentionally, making contented little noises.

# CHAPTER 11

"I thank you for your assistance," Balgair told his benefactor as the carriage rocked and swayed along the dirt track, heading away from the prison.

"I may have had at least a little choice in the matter," came the reply, "And, then again, I had no choice at all."

"You chose to help me."

"I felt compelled to help you. It's not the same thing."

"That is a strange thing to experience," Balgair admitted, "I have felt it myself."

"There are more things in this world, and in the world beyond this world, than we could ever begin to imagine."

"Those are words that I have heard before."

"They are words that date back a long time," replied the man.

"There are other words that date back a long time, as well."

"There are, indeed."

"Special words?" asked Balgair.

"Yes."

"Words that bind a person to a cause?" suggested Balgair.

"Tell me," the man enquired, "Do you believe in The Quickening?"

"I do."

"The Quickening is like the head of a bear, poking out of the bushes," the man began, "When we look at the bushes and we see the bear's head, we can have no doubt that there is a bear's body attached to it."

"You are talking dangerously," warned Balgair.

"If you believe in The Quickening, then I have to suspect that you believe in something else. Something gravely important to the future of Scotland. I have to suspect that you believe in a struggle that has continued since the days of the Vikings."

"Now you are talking *extremely* dangerously indeed," Balgair cautioned.

"I think you have declared yourself too far, already, to be suffering a sudden bout of shyness."

"You know the penalty for treason?"

"Death," the man answered.

"And that does not worry you?"

"If I must die for my beliefs, then I must die."

"You must believe in something very important."

"My life would be hollow, empty and without meaning," replied the man, leaning forward with earnest enthusiasm, "If it were conducted other than in loyalty to my cause."

Balgair paused, giving serious consideration to his next words, before he spoke them.

"You mean *our* cause," he said.

"Men with such a cause would be dead men if they were to be discovered."

"I am a man escaping from a prison," Balgair observed, wryly, "In there, I was already as good as dead."

"For a murder you did not commit."

"How do *you* know why I was in there?" Balgair demanded, "And how could you possibly know that I am innocent?"

"Because it was I who put you there."

*"What?"* exclaimed Balgair, beginning to rise from his seat.

"We are Brydda, you and I, and I could not risk our enemies reaching you with their assassins."

Balgair slumped back down and looked astounded.

"This coach," the man continued, "Will take you to Stirling. You will be safe there. From Stirling, you will be taken back to your Clan Lands."

Balgair nodded, feeling dazed.

"My coach is yours. I will get out of it when we reach the crossroads. Three heavily armed guards will get in. They will protect you."

"Why are you doing this?"

"Because I must, for the sake of Scotland."

"Have these recent days been as baffling for you as they have been for me?"

"Yes!" the big, tall, well-dressed man grinned, "They have!"

"I need to tell you something."

The man raised an eyebrow.

"I have seen the flames," said Balgair.

"The flames of legend?"

"Yes."

"I envy you. You are blessed."

"I feel blessed, but I don't know why they would choose to appear to me."

"You must answer the call," the man said, as if it were entirely obvious, "You must do what you must do."

"And what is it I must do?"

"You must protect the queen, I believe," the man advised, "You must protect Queen Annis, Queen of the West."

"You know this?"

"I feel this."

"I don't understand. I am as likely to meet Queen Annis as I am to meet Kiffan the Defiant!"

"You may be eight centuries too late to meet Kiffan the Defiant, but if the power that has been sent into this world to bring about Our Maker's will, intends you to meet Queen Annis, then meet her you most certainly will."

"You say this truly?"

"I do," the man confirmed.

Balgair nodded, thoughtfully, and it was clear that the man was convinced.

"Wait!" Balgair demanded, "You said that it was *you* who put me in jail!"

"I did."

"Then what are you? Surely not a judge?" Balgair protested, "For I was never brought to court under the King's Justice. I was accused of my crime, by people I had never met before, while I sat in chains in the back of a prison wagon."

"I am not a judge. I am not a magistrate. Such people, here abouts, are all corrupt. If it were up to them, they would have sent you to the gallows without a moment's delay. It would not have been the inside of a prison cell you would have seen, but the inside of a hangman's hood."

"Then who are you? A Lord? A Duke?"

"Oh! So, if I am not a corrupt judge or magistrate, then I am one of those who corrupt them, am I?"

"I would know who you are, Sir, if you will tell me, please?"

The man laughed, first aloud, and then to himself.

"I was told, recently – under strange circumstances – that whatever needs to be, will be."

"Strange circumstances?" Balgair asked.

The man laughed again, the amusement in his eyes finding his mouth and placing a huge grin on it.

"If I told you what I meant, and the thing that has happened to me, you would think me insane."

"If I told you the things that have happened to me," Balgair challenged, "Then you would not merely *think* me insane, you would be absolutely *convinced* of it!"

They both laughed heartily, slapping their thighs and clapping their hands with glee.

"Those words I spoke, which were a quotation," the man confided, "Were said to me by an unexpected visitor to my study, late yesterday evening."

Balgair leaned forward and looked expectant, eager to hear this tale.

"The visitor of whom I speak was, at one moment, not there, and then – the very next moment – they were most assuredly there. I quickly jumped to my feet and checked my door and I found it to be firmly locked. I rushed to my window and checked that, too. It was solidly bolted and impossible to open. I swiftly moved to my fireplace and confirmed for myself that the flames were too high, and the heat going up the chimney too intense, for anybody to have entered that way."

Balgair nodded, completely enthralled.

"It was as if my visitor had appeared out of thin air!"

"Then later," Balgair suggested, "She disappeared, right before your eyes, in the very same fashion?"

"Yes!" he cried, "She did! Exactly so!"

Balgair smiled, his suspicions fully confirmed.

"Wait!" the man objected, "I never mentioned that my visitor was female!"

"She was a little girl, wasn't she?"

"Yes! You're right!" gasped the man, "How could you know that?"

"I felt her presence from my prison cell. I called to her and spoke to her, repeatedly and insistently, eventually gaining her attention. Then, not long after that, she appeared."

"In my case," the man revealed, "I felt only the vaguest possible presence and I spoke not one word to her. I most certainly didn't call to her. She took me by surprise and made me almost leap out of my britches and hit my head on the ceiling!"

They both laughed, again, but – very soon – the man's face became grave and serious.

"The little girl who appeared in my study told me things. One of those things was that my memory would play tricks on me. She said that there would be things that I would remember when the time was right, but that they would completely evade me when it was not. She told me that, when the time came, I would always know what to do and when to do it."

"I see," said Balgair, making no effort to hide the fact that he didn't.

"She said that you would know me, but only when the time to know me had come."

Balgair blinked, as if seeing the man for the first time.

"I *do* know you! You are the Constable," he blurted, "She spoke of you. She said that you and I were of the same faith. I cannot understand how I could not have recognised you, especially when you spoke of The Quickening and..."

"Mine is not the only memory playing tricks, then?"

"No, it most certainly is not."

"There is one thing that is sad. I must admit that, now, for it causes me a pang of sorrow."

"What is that?"

"She said that for the sake of the cause and for the safety of all involved, once we parted at the crossroads, neither you nor

I would know each other any longer and it would be as if we had never met."

"That is, indeed, a pity."

"I cannot for the life of me think how she could have known that the crossroads would, indeed, be the place where we would end up parting."

There was a shout from the driver, perched on top of the carriage, and the constable responded by tapping the metal end of his cane against the roof.

"We are here," the constable said, "This is the crossroads."

"Thank you for your help, Sir," said Balgair, extending his hand, " I mean that sincerely."

Balgair's hand was taken and shaken, enthusiastically.

"In answer to your earlier question: I am Ewan Burberry, Constable of Edinburgh, appointed by King James these past two years."

"I am Balgair McRory, former member of The MacDonald Cavalry."

"You mean former and future member of The MacDonald Cavalry."

"If fate blesses me for it to be so."

The carriage came to a halt and the two men got out. There, they hugged and slapped each other on the back, like old friends, then shook hands, again.

"I believe that our paths will cross again," said the constable.

"I hope so."

"So do I, very much."

"It will be strange not knowing you."

"Strange and sad."

Balgair got back up into the coach and deposited himself into a seat. Leaning up against the window, he idly took in the scenery, gazing this way and that. His eyes eventually found a well attired gentleman climbing into the saddle of a horse.

The driver of the coach leaned down from his seat with practised precariousness.

"Just so that you know, Sir," he shouted, "We are going a little way along this road to the junction, where we have a group of soldiers to pick up for the journey to Stirling."

"Thank you for letting me know," replied Balgair, still watching the man on the horse.

Just as the driver urged the horses forward, Balgair addressed him in a loud whisper: "Who is the man on the horse?"

"He travelled with us from Edinburgh," lied the driver, already having been prepared and rehearsed for this eventuality, "But he slept the whole of the way here, so you'll not have had the chance to talk to him."

Balgair watched as the stranger turned his horse to head south and kept his eyes on him until he was out of sight. Balgair could not shake the feeling that there was something about him that was oddly familiar.

# CHAPTER 12

Greesha blinked at the sunlight pouring in through the tiny window of her tiny cabin and shaded her eyes with her hands. The sun's glare on the sea was so intense she could hardly see anything beyond it.

It wasn't until the boat began to turn sharply inland that she was able to make out the view. They were close to the craggy, boulder strewn hills of Ellan Vannin and the sea was crashing up and over the savagely rocky coastline with relentless waves, capped with frothing, white swells.

After several minutes of buffeting and rolling, the boat hit calmer water and she could see the golden sand of the beach come into view. Before long, she heard the thud as the underside of the vessel struck the shore, causing it to judder to a halt.

Almost the entire crew clambered off the boat and onto the sand, taking with them the thick ropes that were attached to the prow. The ropes had wooden poles tied through them at intervals and the men applied themselves to these to haul the boat further up the sand. Once this had been accomplished, the captain and his first officer disembarked. A few seconds later, somebody knocked on Greesha's door. Upon answering it, she was motioned to join everyone ashore.

As soon as she had climbed off the boat, Asif beckoned her to join him.

"I wish to talk," he said, sitting them down on some smooth, flat rocks under an old, gnarled tree.

"As you wish," she replied, happy to be shaded from the fierce sun.

"The men will work," he said, "We will watch. I have worked very hard for many years. I have earned the privilege."

A question hung in the air. The question was obvious. Greesha declined to leave it there.

"And I?" she asked.

"And you have saved all of our lives, so you, too, have earned the privilege."

"I merely asked that it should happen."

"You asked and you were answered."

There was a long, brooding silence during which Asif said nothing, but made a dozen different faces of contemplation, of disappointment, of annoyance and of exasperation. Greesha patiently held her tongue.

"The man who sold you. He was your father?"

"Yes."

"You must hate him."

"No."

"He sold you. You are obliged to hate him."

"I have forgiven him."

"How can you forgive someone who sells you like a basket of apples?"

"I had become a burden to my family in many ways. By what I said. By how I behaved. By the claims I made. I told them that I had begun to see faeries. It all brought them trouble and shame. In the end, my father did what life and circumstances forced him to do."

"I do not think I could forgive my father if he had sold me."

"The money your captain gave him will likely put food on the table for my family for several weeks."

"Even still…"

"People had begun to look at me strangely. They were worried about me. Some were even fearful of me. It would not have been long before they had started saying that I might be a witch. How much longer, beyond that, would it have been before they tied me to a post and burned me alive?"

"So, when all things have been considered," said Asif, scratching his chin and arching an eyebrow, "By selling you, your father may well have done you a service by saving your life."

"Yes."

"I was making a joke," he protested.

"When we jest," she said, squinting up at him, "We make it possible to say the most serious of things."

"You are a healer, a dabbler in miracles and, now, you are a philosopher!" He laughed.

"And I am fluent in Arabic," she added.

"Yes, that too," Asif grinned, "Which means that we have not met – you and I – by accident."

"You believe it is fate?"

"I believe that you are not a six year old girl, even though that is how you appear. I believe you are some kind of an angel in human form."

"At least my only offence was seeing faeries. I had not progressed to angels!" she teased, "Perhaps it is not *me* who deserves to be burned."

They both laughed, but Asif suddenly stiffened and turned. Following the direction of his eyes, Greesha saw that the captain was approaching them.

"Captain Bashri," said Asif, rising and bowing to him.

"Asif," said the captain, returning the bow.

The two sat in uncomfortable silence as the captain looked meaningfully from his First Officer, across to Greesha, and then back again. It was clearly a look of censure.

"Why is this girl not working?" asked the captain, finally.

"It is not fitting that she should, at the moment."

Greesha looked at the two men from the corner of her eye, studying them as best she could. She took careful note of their posture and their tone of voice. There was something out of place. It was in the manner of their interaction, she decided. Their relationship was not what it pretended to be. Supposedly, one was the superior and the other was the junior, but their conversation had been more like one between equals.

"She is a child," the captain said, "I bought her to work. She should be working."

"She is assisting me in an urgent matter," Asif responded.

Captain Bashir looked sharply at Greesha, unable to disguise his shock.

"She is but a child," the captain scoffed.

"It is this child who has kept us all alive," said Asif, tersely.

The captain grunted in disgust, rose to his feet and strode off without a word.

Asif allowed the tense atmosphere to disperse before he spoke.

"Do you believe in a god?" he asked.

"I believe in the only God."

"How do you know that there is only one?"

"Because there *is* only one."

The man gave a long, forlorn sigh before replying.

"That's only what you believe. You cannot know."

"The truth has reached me through generations and, far back enough, that those generations lived in a time when they knew God and when His miracles were commonplace. A time when He was not hidden from us."

"My father believes in the Jew who was crucified in Jerusalem."

"But this, in itself, is not the cause of your despair."

"In my country I am not only a merchant, but a nobleman, and my father is a Provincial Ruler."

"But that isn't the cause of your despair."

Asif shook his head.

"My father's highest court of law has a man in custody whom they would put to death for blasphemy. That man's beliefs are the same as my father's beliefs."

"So if that man is guilty of blasphemy, then your father is also guilty of blasphemy?"

"Exactly so."

"And the penalty for such a crime?"

"The penalty is death."

"That is the cause of your despair."

To her surprise Asif, again, shook his head.

"My father, as our laws permit, has appointed me to be this man's judge. On my return from this voyage, I must give my judgement."

"*Now* we have it," exclaimed Greesha, "In judging this man, you also judge your father."

Asif applauded her.

"Yes. If my judgement is that he is guilty, then so is my father."

"What is the man's blasphemy?"

"He believes in three gods, not the one, true God."

"The sign of this man's faith? Is it the symbol of a fish?"

"Yes, it is, and the cross, too," said Asif, placing his hands so that his fingers demonstrated the sign he meant.

"Well, that is simple then," Greesha announced.

"It is?"

"Yes. He simply lacks the ability to explain his belief."

"Do you understand his belief?"

"Yes."

"But he is a heretic."

"No. He is merely confused," she answered, smiling.

"You make light of this?" scowled Asif.

"No," she said, looking deliberately serious and contrite.

Asif sighed, again, and hung his head in his hands. Greesha drew in a long breath and then blew it out slowly through the tiny "O" she had made with her lips. This forced her cheeks to puff out and made a noise. Asif looked up as he heard it and Greesha promptly rubbed her hands as if in preparation for a task.

"He believes," she observed, "In God as being one, but – yet – as three."

Asif looked disappointed, having hoped for some kind of inspiration from her. Picking up a pebble, Greesha leaned and washed it in a little rivulet of water that ran close by her feet.

"If I place this pebble on my left palm," she asked, making that exact motion, "How many pebbles do I have?"

"You have one," Asif replied, glumly.

"If I place the pebble on my right palm," she asked, repositioning the pebble, accordingly, "How many pebbles do I have?"

"One."

"If I place the pebble on the tip of my tongue, how many pebbles do I have?" she inquired, sitting the little stone as described and wishing that she had washed it a little more rigorously.

"One."

"So, the people of this man's faith believe in a God who is God Himself and who is also God as a spirit and who is also God in the form of a man," she enthused.

Asif gave her a look of disgust.

"And?" he asked, scornfully.

"And, although the pebble was in three different places, at three different times, there was only ever one pebble."

"And?" asked Asif, no less disgusted.

"And I don't think this explanation is working, is it?"

Asif made a growling noise.

"Because my point," she said, raising her hands in appeal to his better nature, "Is that…."

Asif drew in a huge breath, grimaced and then let it out in the longest, most prolonged and most mournful sigh she had ever heard.

"Don't do that again," she beseeched him, sensing that he might not really be as annoyed as he seemed, "Because you placed yourself at serious risk of blowing yourself completely inside out!"

He grinned at her, but the grin quickly faded, his heart not being fully in it.

"I did not tell you that the man who faces almost certain death is my lifelong friend," said Asif, "Whatever my decision and whatever the fate of them both, it must be made justly and without favour."

"I understand."

"You are a slave," said Asif, "The captain owns you. You are his property. You face a life ahead of you of drudgery and misery. If you can solve this terrible problem that I face, I give you my word that I will set you free. You will have your liberty."

"I understand."

Asif went back to hanging his head in his hands and Greesha adopted a respectful silence.

Several minutes passed, then Greesha abruptly clapped her hands, gripped by inspiration. The noise was louder than she had intended and caused Asif to jump.

"I have it, this time!" she announced.

He looked at her imploringly, his expression begging her not to raise his hopes, only to dash them for a second time.

"I genuinely believe that I have an explanation," she insisted.

Asif shrugged his shoulders to show his lack of enthusiasm.

"Imagine that someone went to the captain and delivered to him a letter, written for his attention. If you were to ask him who brought him the letter, what might he say?"

"A messenger."

"Imagine that the same person went to a member of your crew who had a wound that would not heal. Imagine that they applied a paste of herbs to the wound to help it heal. If you were to ask that crew member who tended to their wound, what might they say?"

"A healer."

"Imagine that the very same person who brought the letter and who dressed the wound went to someone and showed them how to tie a particular knot or draw a particular character or perform some difficult arithmetic. If you were to ask that person who showed them how to do that thing, what might they say?"

"A teacher."

"It was the same person. It was not three different people. It was the same person. Yet one man said that they were a messenger, the other said that they were a healer and the last one said that they were a teacher. Were there three people or was there only the one?"

"Only the one."

"Your friend and your father believe in the God who is God Himself?"

"Yes."

"Is the one God that very God?"

"Yes."

"Your friend and your father believe in God who, when He wishes to inspire the world, is said to inhabit this realm as a Spirit. The Spirit of God. The Holy Spirit?"

"Yes," replied Asif, uncertainly.

"The Holy Spirit of God is that very same, single God. Is He none other but the one God?"

"Yes. As far as I know and as far as I would suppose, He is."

"Your friend and your father believe in the God who was not satisfied to only preach to his people from above, telling them that they must be good, without ever knowing or experiencing their temptation and their situation. That God allowed His spirit – the part of him that is His soul – to pass into a man born of this world at the instant of his birth, so that He would not be God beyond and outside this world, but God *within* this world. Am I right?"

"Yes. You are right."

"The man who was the messenger and who was the healer and who was the teacher was just one man. Am I correct?"

"Yes."

"The one God has always been and will always be Himself. The one God who, in spirit, inspires the world is the very same God. The one God who delivered His soul into a man's body to know this world, is the very same God."

"Yes! Yes! Yes! You are right!"

"Do you have a wife, Asif?"

"Yes, I do."

"Do you have children, Asif?"

"Yes, I have a daughter."

"Your father calls you son?"

"Yes."

"Your wife calls you Husband?"

"Yes."

"Your daughter calls you father?"

"Yes."

"How can that be? For there is only one Asif."

Asif leapt to his feet, cupped his hands around his mouth and bellowed to the captain and the crew.

"She is free!" he cried, "She is no longer a slave! She is free! Listen! Listen to me! All of you! She has her liberty! She is free!"

# CHAPTER 13

Greesha inhaled deeply and filled her lungs with the salty air as Glasgow appeared around the bend of the river. She would soon be in the Kingdom of Strathclyde, which – one day, she knew – would be part of a Greater Scotland. This is where her instincts told her to be. This is where she had been drawn to go.

As their boat pulled down its sails and put out its oars to approach the nearest of the stout, wooden piers, she noticed a group of three Viking longships a little further along the riverbank.

"You need not fear the Vikings, here," said Asif, encouragingly, "These people are traders, not attackers."

"I do not fear them," she replied.

"The Vikings are fierce and they enjoy spilling blood."

"They know the truth about death."

"What is that?"

"They know that death is not the end of life. That knowledge makes them bold."

"It makes them crazy!"

Asif supervised as their boat came to the pier. It was tied up with stout ropes and, at strategic points, wooden ramps were tethered between gaps in the deck rails. Once he was happy with their moorings, Asif organised the crew to begin unloading their cargo. As the process got under way, he took Greesha to sit in the shade, on some wooden barrels, over which a sailcloth canopy had been erected.

Asif instructed that certain kegs were to be stacked beside them, out of the sun, and that extra care should be taken with the handling of them.

"These are for a special customer," he told her, nodding in the direction of the man who was walking towards them from the middle distance.

"Does he buy a lot from you?"

"He buys the very best that I have."

"He looks like he is a good man."

"You can tell that?" asked Asif, before correcting himself, "Yes, of course you can tell!"

"I want to ask a kindness of you, if I may?"

"There is nothing that you can ask that I would not give if it were within my power," Asif enthused, "For you have saved both my best friend and my father from death."

"You may not be pleased with my request."

"Ask it, none-the-less, and it will be granted."

"I want you to sell me to that man as a slave."

"What?" gasped Asif, "How could you ask such a thing? I have set you free!"

"What would you do to save the life of your wife or your daughter?"

"I would do absolutely anything," he said, before suddenly raising his hand to caution her and leaning close, "You *know* that I would do anything for them and for you. You *know* about things that you cannot know."

"I know that you are the finest father your daughter could have ever hoped to have in a dozen lifetimes."

Asif squirmed with embarrassment.

"I know that your wife could never have met a finer man."

Asif raised a hand to cover his mouth and his eyes became misty. Greesha knew him to be on the verge of tears so, to distract him, she dropped to her knees and lowered her head.

"Yes, Master, I understand," she said, loudly.

Asif looked puzzled for a fleeting moment, but then realised that the man who was his best customer, had just come within hearing range.

"Little girl," said Asif, also in a loud voice, "You are worth more than a dozen slaves. You have no equal."

"Good slaves are hard to come by," said John Merricroft, coming to stand beside them.

"My good friend!" said Asif, in Arabic, greeting his best customer with genuine warmth, "It is so good to see you, again!"

The two men shook hands, bowed to each other and then hugged.

"Good slaves are like gold," said John, in perfect Arabic, eyeing Greesha as he spoke.

"They are! They are, indeed!" agreed Asif, "As long as you beat them hard enough."

John looked shocked, but then broke into a smile and laughed.

"I know for certain, Asif, that you do *not* beat your slaves. Just as you know, full well, that I do not beat mine."

"This one is such a credit to me," said Asif, sadly, as he fondly stroked the hair of his newly, self-appointed slave, "I feel very proud of her, but…"

"But what?" asked the other man, looking curious.

"But in my country, back in Morocco, the flies give her such fevers and she suffers so badly from them. I fear that I cannot put her through the hardship of taking her back with me after this voyage is over."

John looked sympathetically at Greesha and his face was filled with genuine concern.

"I could take her from you, Asif, if you would wish it."

"Would you, my friend? I would be beyond grateful."

"Slaves are not so very different to either you or I, Asif. It is purely a quirk of fate that we are not in their place and they are not in ours," said John in a low voice, looking around to check that nobody might be overhearing his scandalous and subversive opinions.

"I do not think you need fear people listening, John. There are precious few Arabic speakers around here!" Asif jibed, shoving his friend playfully in the shoulder with his fist.

John performed a little pantomime where he took up the cowering and furtive stance of a man fearful of detection and made as if to hide behind the stack of barrels.

"You can never be too sure," he cautioned, before bellowing with laughter.

Asif slapped him on the back and the two men exchanged hugs, again. Greesha, for her part, stood placidly by, her eyes cast towards the ground.

"I will take this little girl and I will look after her well," John announced, patting her shoulder.

Asif looked towards Greesha and his lip trembled with emotion. John, wishing not to intrude, quickly turned to the side and pretended to waft away a very persistent – but wholly imaginary – fly.

Asif crouched on his haunches and wrapped his slave in a hug, a tear escaping and rolling down his cheek as he did so.

"Who is raising this dust?" cried John, flapping a hand and feigning a fit of coughing, "It is all over."

With this John duly brushed his friend's clothing to enhance the illusion.

"Goodness! It is in the eyes of us both!" complained John, wiping an invisible tear from his own cheek and, then, reaching and wiping a real one from Asif's.

Asif did not speak, fearing that his voice might break, but tousled Greesha's hair and tweaked her nose, affectionately.

"How much do you want for this girl?" asked John, making his tone sound as offhand and casual as he could, "What is the price?"

Asif looked troubled, as he had not even considered this aspect of the transaction.

"What is her name?" asked John, in Arabic.

Asif tried to clear his throat to speak, but found it a challenge.

"If it pleases you, Sir," replied the slave, helpfully, in Arabic, "My name is Greesha. I am something like six years of age, but I am unsure. I may, in truth, be seven or even eight. I was born on the island of Ellan Vannin."

"You have learned Arabic!" said John Merricroft, "You have learned it well! You are a credit to your master."

Greesha bowed low and, then – for good measure – added a curtsey.

"Tell me, little girl," her prospective owner asked, switching from Arabic into English, "Can you understand me, now?"

"I can, Sir, yes," she replied, in English.

"But you will have no idea what I am saying, this time?" he asked, using Scottish Gaelic.

"I have no more clue what you are saying than a fish would have if it found itself up a tree," she replied, in the same tongue, with a perfect turn of phrase, and with a lovely smile.

"Asif, she is a little miracle! She is polite and well mannered. She is quick witted and intelligent. She has a pleasantness and charm to her, too."

"My master will confirm that I also have talents as a healer."

"A healer? At such a young age? This is extraordinary. I am most impressed."

Asif nodded eagerly, to confirm her abilities, but could not manage to speak. John patted his arm. It was obvious to him that his friend's attachment to the girl was a deep one and that parting with her was causing him pain.

Reaching into his cloak, John produced a leather purse, which he proceeded to untie. From the purse he assembled a small stack of coins and handed them to Greesha's owner.

"I think you will find this sum to be sufficient, even for a slave as gifted as this one."

Asif was compelled to agree. The sum he had been given was, indeed, a large one. It was far more than he would have ever demanded.

John looked at Asif and saw the look of desolation on his face. He knew that even a hundred silver coins would not make this sale any easier for his friend. John knew that to decline the purchase of the girl would cause Asif even more grief, compelling him to sell her to somebody else whom he did not know and could not entirely trust. Just then a thought came to him. It was, he congratulated himself, a perfect solution.

*'When is a slave not a slave?'* he asked himself, *'When they are not a slave,'* came his own reply.

Just as Asif was about to insist on handing back one of the coins, his friend did something remarkable.

"What is this?" asked John, reaching behind Greesha's ear and appearing to take a silver coin from it, "You wish to buy your freedom, little girl?"

Asif looked startled for a moment, but his face quickly erupted into a grin as he realised his friend's generous intention.

"Then, I am happy to accept," John told Greesha, turning the coin over in his hand and pretending to marvel at it, "For this is a mighty sum for such a tiny person."

With these words, he dropped the silver piece into his purse. Nobody said a word about it, but all three knew that this was the very place from which it had just come.

"You are now free, little girl," he told Greesha, lifting his face to the sky, "Praise God."

Asif and Greesha took advantage of the moment to exchange a conspiratorial glance, for they both knew that this was her second taste of freedom that day.

"That would be very kind of you," she replied in Arabic, before adding, in English, "Liberty, though it tastes most sweet, will do nothing to fill my belly."

Her potential employer narrowed his eyes at her, warily, and looked at her with an expression that was on the very brink of suspicion.

"You speak many languages and in a manner that is at odds with your age. I would swear you to be seven, but your way of talking has me thinking that you are, at the very least, another fifteen years beyond that."

Greesha studiously hid her alarm, while cursing herself for her clumsy mistake.

"Her father," Asif invented, "Was most keen upon debate and discussion. He and his friends would talk long into the night. She would often fall asleep listening to them, absorbing every word."

John's expression was momentarily baffled, before he quickly banished it behind a broad smile.

"Well, little one, let me assure you that I had no intention of casting you onto the streets as a penniless waif. Nothing was further from my mind."

Greesha looked at him, pensively, hanging on his every word.

"You see, now that you are no longer a slave, little girl, I wish to make you an offer of employment."

Greesha beamed at him.

"I need someone who will take care of my father. Since he lost the use of his legs, he has confined himself to the warehouse, refusing to do the thing he loves, which is to travel around promoting and selling our goods."

"I remember the accident," said Asif, "He fell from a horse, did he not?"

"Yes, he did," John confirmed, preferring this false version of events to the truth of what had actually happened, "My father's fall has set a dark cloud over his life. The people who come to buy at the warehouse sense his sombre moods and, despite my best efforts, it has begun to impact on our trade."

"He was an active man," said Asif, "He was fit and healthy, especially for his age. It must be difficult for him."

"It is," John replied, "And he has my every sympathy. I feel for him. I only wish that I could snap my fingers and make him walk."

Absentmindedly, Greesha looked at her hand. The proposition appeared to fascinate her. With a look of thoughtful contemplation, she opened her palm and touched the tip of her thumb and middle finger together. Asif caught the motion and, shooting her a look of reprimand, hurriedly grasped her hand and put it back by her side.

"Don't even think about it," whispered Asif, placing his lips close to her ear, "Well, at least not yet," he added, smiling at his friend, John, reassuringly.

Asif motioned to two members of his crew and they came along the pier to attend him. He pointed to the cargo that had been stacked for his premium customer and indicated that it should be loaded into the spice merchant's wagon. They set about this task without delay.

"I should caution you, little girl," warned John, "That my father is... How shall I say?"

"Cantankerous?" suggested Greesha.

John blinked in surprise.

"Yes. He is exactly that," he agreed, "But how could you know?"

"And how could you dare to say it?" added Asif, nudging her gently in the ribs.

"The word just came into my head," she replied, smiling sweetly.

"Perhaps," suggested Asif, "You should have left it there."

"No," John interrupted, "She is fine. I would not wish her to be timid. I prefer that she has a little spirit about her."

Greesha gave Asif a wink and, speaking to him in a whisper far too loud for secrecy said: "Because she's going to need it."

John threw his head back and roared with laughter. Within a heartbeat, Asif was laughing, too. Greesha, unable to restrain herself, joined in. The sound of Greesha's laughter caused both men to laugh even louder. Before long, they were all helpless.

It took a few minutes for the little party to fully recover themselves and involved several relapses along the way.

Finally, with the wagon now loaded, they assembled to make their farewells.

"Take good care of her," Asif insisted.

"I will," her new employer assured him, "I give you my word."

"Be good and make me proud," Asif told Greesha, giving her yet another final hug.

"Live for a long time and prosper well," she replied.

John embraced Asif and slapped him on the back.

"I will see you on your next visit to Glasgow in three months' time, Asif," he said, "When you arrive with my next supply of the finest spices."

"You will, indeed, and, John, please give my very best regards to your father."

"I will, my friend. He will be sad to have missed you."

Greesha closed her eyes for a brief moment and, then, spoke what came into her head.

"He will be very sad. Very sad indeed, in fact. It would have cheered him greatly to have seen you."

The two men turned to her in unison, then looked at each other with shared puzzlement.

"It is true, but how do you know that?" asked John.

"However she knows it," quipped Asif, "She seems to know it."

"Is there no end to her talents?"

"If there is, John, then I did not discover it."

The two men chuckled.

"Very well," said the spice merchant to his supplier, "It seems that you are invited to dinner, this evening, my friend."

"I'm sorry, but I will miss the tide. I need to leave."

John looked disappointed. Asif looked at Greesha for guidance. After a moment, so did John. Greesha closed her eyes for a couple of seconds, then smiled.

"You will not be delayed if you leave on the morning tide," she promised.

"Then I am delighted to accept your invitation, John," Asif grinned.

John nodded slowly, mulling over what had just happened, intrigued by his friend's instantaneous and unquestioning acceptance of the little girl's advice.

The spice merchant's carriage, which had been parked beyond his wagon, was brought around by its driver. Once aboard, John and Asif promptly began to exchange tales of recent events in their lives and recollections of old times that they had shared.

Greesha leaned into the corner of the sumptuous vehicle, snuggling against a cushion, and feigned sleep.

# CHAPTER 14

Balgair McRory eyed his fellow travellers in the coach as casually as he could, not wishing to draw their attention or provoke their animosity. Despite his care, it did not escape their notice. The man who, of the three, appeared to be their leader, addressed him directly:

"You are going home?" he asked.

"Yes, I am," replied Balgair in surprise, "How could you know that?"

"This coach has but one purpose. That purpose is to convey you on your way. The three of us also have but one purpose. Our purpose is to ensure that you reach your destination alive and well."

Balgair looked around the coach, taking in its fine upholstery, the decorative elements added to the carving of its fixtures and the quality of its carpet and roof lining. Why had he not noticed this before? Had the drama of escaping from prison managed to scramble his brains? This was certainly no public coach plying a route for paying passengers. It was far too grand for that. This was someone's personal property and – beyond that – something in which they took pride.

"Do you know me?" Balgair asked the man.

"I know something of you," came the reply, "But it is precious little and, frankly, my interest extends very little further than the silver pieces in my coin sock that have paid me and my men to keep any Campbell a good distance from you."

"Why Campbells?"

"Why them?" the man challenged, "Because those who know things – and whose words can be trusted far beyond common rumour – are of the opinion that the Campbells are plotting something."

"Plotting something? Why would that put me in danger?"

"Think on it for a moment, will you?" he invited, "If the Campbells are up to no good, then a glimpse of that kilt of yours would have a Campbell's dirk to your throat in an instant!"

Balgair looked down at himself and, taking in The MacDonald tartan adorning his legs, he grunted his acknowledgement.

"The MacDonald has sent you?" he enquired.

"No, not he."

"Then who?"

"Someone else. An enemy of your enemies."

"An enemy of my enemies, you say? How do I know that *you* are not Campbells yourselves!"

"There are three of us. We are all of a goodly size, like yourself, and yet you're still alive, despite you being unarmed."

Balgair jolted in panic and reached for where he might openly carry a blade, but found nothing. He searched, urgently, within his clothing, but remained empty-handed.

"I'm told," the man smirked, "That the Campbells favour outnumbering their foe by four-to-one, but I'd say that even a trio of Campbells would be happy to tussle with you, under the circumstances."

Balgair's mind reeled. He was in a carriage with three men he didn't know and he had no weapon. Had he taken leave of his senses?

"Who has hired you?" Balgair demanded.

"Someone who wishes you well."

"Someone of influence?"

"Someone who would remain anonymous."

"Why?"

"They pay me well. I do as I am told and I don't ask them questions. It is none of my business. I cannot help you."

Balgair nodded, thoughtfully, as he mulled over their conversation.

"I'll pry no more, then," said Balgair, at last, "But I'd ask you to be good enough – if you are truly not my foes – to let me have a sword. I feel naked without one."

The man nodded and, taking out a dagger, used the handle of it to knock on the roof of the coach. The coach promptly slowed and stopped.

The man got out and spoke with the driver for a moment, before going to the rear of the coach and opening the stowage box, there. A few moments later, he appeared at the door with something wrapped in oiled cloth.

"If you'll take a look at this," the man said, holding out the bundle to Balgair, "I think it will meet with your approval."

Balgair laid the bundle across his lap and pulled loose the cord twisted around it. As the man climbed back into the coach, Balgair unrolled the bundle to reveal its contents. On seeing them, he gave a cry of surprise.

"My sword!" he exclaimed, "The one that was taken from me!"

The man grinned, sharing his delight.

"Where did you get this?" asked Balgair.

The man made a face and shook his head. Balgair knew better than to question him further on the subject.

"I have a sword and you three have not," Balgair observed, "How would you fend off an attack?"

All three men, simultaneously, reached down to the wooden panels beneath the front of their seats. As each released a hidden catch, the doors fell open. Attached to the inside of them was an impressive array of swords, daggers, pistols and powder horns.

Their leader, sat opposite Balgair, slipped his hand into a pocket of his seat and produced from it what was commonly known as a 'Donkey's Hoof'. This was a tough leather bag filled with half a dozen lead balls. Such a thing was a devastatingly effective weapon at close quarters.

"We also have one of these, each," announced their leader, "I've seen one take a man's ear clean off the side of his head with no more effort than wiping milk from a counter."

His words were not threatening, Balgair decided. They were more playful or confiding than anything else, so he grinned back mischievously.

"Many an ale house landlord has successfully sorted out a disorderly customer with one of those!" Balgair replied.

This comment was greeted with much laughter and each man started to testify to a grizzly instance of a Donkey's Hoof being used.

The rest of the journey was spent in the amiable telling of stories and recounting of adventures.

# CHAPTER 15

As the coach arrived in Stirling, Balgair McRory suddenly realised how hungry he had been. His armed escort obligingly took him to an inn where the owner, without question and without request for payment, furnished them with a hearty meal.

"Your credit is good here, I gather?" Balgair asked the leader of his guards.

"It is not my credit, but that of my employer," the man advised, "And it is good in a whole lot of places."

"He must be a worthy individual."

"They know that he will settle his account without delay."

"He is a good employer?"

The guard looked at Balgair suspiciously for a few seconds before answering.

"I am more than happy to work for him when he asks. So are my men," he replied, nodding towards the two guards who had gone to sit at a table by the fireplace.

"Your employer has my gratitude."

The man looked around, clearly on edge.

"It would be best if you were to talk more quietly and to mention nothing of any substance."

"Are we in danger?" Balgair whispered.

"No danger. Our only risk is of wagging tongues."

"I see."

"The business of anyone is the business of everyone, in places like this."

Balgair leaned closer, to talk confidentially, but the man held up a hand to stop him.

"Whatever you are about to say," he cautioned, "Is best not said."

Balgair sat back in his chair and tucked into his food, their meals having just arrived.

"On the way here," he announced, obediently changing the topic, "I was bitten by the biggest Croggin I have ever seen."

His dining companion laughed.

"Aye. They are the worst kind of flies," he replied.

"Some people complain of those tiny wee flies, but its those huge beasts that annoy me."

"The small ones are a nuisance," the man agreed, "But the big ones, they want to go to war with us!"

They both laughed and smiled, sharing the distraction from the previous tension. They ate their fill of their meals without further conversation and Balgair managed to get through two flagons of ale. There was no doubt that the inn and its customers were friendly enough, but there was a vague undercurrent of unease that it was impossible to ignore.

As they finished eating, Balgair's mind raced as he tried to think of another, equally innocuous, topic for conversation. Before he reached a conclusion, the door to the inn opened, just enough for a face to be seen through the gap. The man beyond the door nodded and the door closed again.

All three of the guards, who had – he now realised – been waiting for this, got to their feet. Balgair did likewise.

"Time to go?" asked Balgair.

Ignoring him, the man at the other side of the table joined the other two guards at the door. To Balgair's surprise they made no attempt to open it. They stood idly, waiting for what Balgair guessed to be around half a minute, at which point there came a single, soft knock on the door. The guard who had sat with him grabbed the handle, pulled open the door and stood, holding it wide, and motioned for everyone to go through.

Outside, a little distance from the inn, stood four horses drinking from a water trough. Without a word, Balgair's three companions each untied a horse and mounted it. Balgair, following their lead, did the same.

The little convoy set off at a steady pace and nobody spoke until they were out of the town. Once they had passed the last of the little houses, their leader drew his horse alongside Balgair's.

"We'll go with you to Callander," he announced, "We'll stop, on the way, at Doune, to rest the horses."

Balgair nodded. They rode on for several minutes without interaction.

"There has been talk," the man said, abruptly, "Reliable talk about things going on."

Balgair wanted to ask: "*What kind of things?*" but realised that the question was more or less to be taken for granted.

"The army garrison," the man continued, "Has had a lot more wagons arriving and leaving than usual, a fair few of them at night. A number have headed north east from Stirling to join the Great North Road."

That road, Balgair knew, ran directly South from Inverness, joining the Scottish Highlands to the Scottish Lowlands across the River Forth at North Queensferry. This, effectively, made it the route from Edinburgh to Inverness. The man offered no more information, so Balgair ruminated over these details for a while.

"I cannot think that the army sending things into the Highlands," Balgair announced, "Is going to be a good thing for the Highlands."

"Aye, too true. Our King of Scotland, who is now also King of England, has moved himself to London. He seems to be very comfortable down there and happy to stay."

"Perhaps the weather is milder?"

"Or perhaps the women are more easily led astray?"

Their group rode on in silence. Reaching Doune, they stopped there – as promised – and watered the horses in a nearby stream before letting them rest a while.

There was something, Balgair decided, that rested heavily on their minds. Responding to their lack of enthusiasm for talk, he did not press them to speak, and they continued their journey with hardly a word.

On reaching the last distance marker for Callander, they encountered a rider heading in the opposite direction. As the rider approached, he gave a shrill whistle. This appeared to confirm him as friendly, for Balgair's escort immediately relaxed.

Without embarking on any pleasantries – not so much as a *'Good morning'* – the rider hurriedly brought his horse close up to them and revealed his news.

"The MacDonalds are here. A lot of them," the man declared, "They all have their jiggies on."

Balgair did not need to be told the implication of this information. A jiggy blanket was designed to cover and warm a man's exposed legs below his kilt, so they must have been getting cold. With the reasonably mild weather, there was only one place that such temperatures would be encountered. That was up in the mountains. If they had taken to the mountains, shunning the main route along the valley floor, it meant that they were going out of their way to avoid being noticed.

Having conveyed his news, the man squinted at Balgair and looked a little uneasy.

"Don't worry. He is, himself, of Clan MacDonald," said the leader of Balgair's escort, nodding towards him, "So, for us, it only remains to be seen if his Clan are happy to see him or if they are going to tie him up with ropes."

Balgair could not stop himself from sitting bolt upright in his saddle, taken aback at this frank assessment of his situation. He had pushed it to the back of his mind.

"It appears that he is uncertain, himself!" laughed the new arrival.

This drew a lot of amusement, but none of it seemed to be unkind.

"If they are bringing rope," Balgair quipped, "It might well be to go around my neck!"

This provoked even more laughter.

"Well," the leader proclaimed, "We are here to protect him from the Clan Campbell and their vile kind, not from his own folk. He had best ride ahead of us, to show our good faith."

Balgair duly walked his steed forward to take position further up the road.

"You are safer staying back there," Balgair joked, "If they fire arrows at me, this far in front, they may well fall short of you."

This was met with a roar of jovial appreciation and a brief ripple of applause for his dark humour.

"If that were my last breakfast," Balgair added, "I am glad to have drunk even more than I ate."

This, too, was met with approval and amiable jibes.

Without further delay, Balgair set off. The rest of them followed, maintaining the discrete distance he had set.

As he rode, Balgair smirked to himself. He had not mentioned to those with him that The MacDonalds would most certainly already be both behind them and to either side, by now, and not just ahead of them.

# CHAPTER 16

As Balgair McRory rounded the next bend in the road, two dozen MacDonald riders came into view, carrying shields and broad swords, split equally on the left and right grass verges. They were sat passively and seemed unconcerned by him appearing.

As he drew nearer, they began to rhythmically thump the inside of their shields with their fists.

There was no mistaking the sound. It was the slow, ominous beat used to conduct a man to the gallows.

# CHAPTER 17

Balgair heard a sound that was very close. It was no more than a handspan from his right ear. It was familiar to him. The sound was Greesha. He was pleased that fate had not yet made him forget her. He didn't bother to turn towards her. He knew that she would not be there. She had just giggled. He felt a twinge of annoyance at her finding his current predicament funny, but he pushed it aside.

Balgair urged his mount forward, for it had sensed the menace in the air and had become a little reluctant. As he closed the space between himself and the 'greeting party', the thudding on their shields grew slightly faster.

After another few horse strides, the drumming became still more rapid.

Presently, with only ten strides of his horse left, the drumming became frantic. In an instant, it was joined by cheering voices. They were whooping, clapping, whistling and rejoicing. He felt a wave of relief flood through him.

As he drew level with them, the riders at either side of the road leapt from their saddles and ran to throng around him. He gawped at them and allowed his hands to be shaken, both left and right. He felt his lower back and thighs being slapped in boisterous congratulations.

After a minute or so, the jubilant mob fell quiet, as if it had been arranged. A horse had emerged from the line of the forest to his left and a single rider came onto the road and halted in the centre. The rider removed his helmet and Balgair recognised him as his father. His father grinned and dismounted. Balgair got down from his own horse and ran to his father's outstretched embrace. They hugged as everyone around them cheered and laughed with glee.

Then, everything became quiet, again. Balgair's father released his son from their hug and stepped back. Balgair looked puzzled.

Another horse came out of the trees, this time from the right. That rider, too, took up a stance in the middle of the road before dismounting to stand on foot. There was absolute silence.

The rider removed his helmet. Balgair gasped. It was The MacDonald himself, the Head of the Clan.

Balgair dropped to one knee and lowered his head.

"Up!" the Clan Chief shouted, "On your feet!"

Balgair obeyed and was startled to find himself being hugged by The MacDonald. The crowd around them erupted into an ecstatic roar.

"My daughter lives because of you, Balgair McRory," The MacDonald shouted in his ear, above the noise, "I owe you her life."

"I did not know her!" Balgair insisted, "I came only to the aid of a woman in distress."

"You came to her aid, one man against several, not knowing the combat skills of your opponents and not knowing if you would survive."

"It was the right thing to do."

"You were the right man for the moment."

Balgair stammered to voice his thanks, but the appropriate words defied him.

The MacDonald raised his hand and, once more, everything returned to silence.

"All hail Balgair McRory!" shouted the Clan Chief.

"Hail! Hail! Hail!" cried the troops, enthusiastically, "Hail Balgair McRory!"

Balgair's heart beat like a drum in his chest and he felt almost dizzy. His father was beaming at him, a smile wrapping round his face from one ear to the other. Balgair beamed back. Then, he saw the look in his father's eyes. His gaze was steady and encouraging. There was more. He was proud and happy, but he was evidently waiting for something else to come.

The MacDonald raised his hand and there was silence. The Leader of their Clan waited, allowing the tension to build and the drama to swell.

"All hail Lieutenant Balgair McRory!" he cried.

All those around them took up the call. Balgair was stunned. He had not even been any rank but that of ordinary cavalryman. His father reached to him, gripped his shoulder and then slapped his back. The MacDonald shook his hand vigorously and then clapped him on both his shoulders, simultaneously.

In his ear, he heard the voice of a little girl.

"Didn't I tell you?" she asked.

# CHAPTER 18

"Who are you?" asked the old man.

"I am somebody," Greesha replied, "And I am nobody."

Grimacing, he rocked his head from side to side, illustrating his indecision.

"Is that not always the way in dreams?" he asked.

"Do dreams not have rules?" she responded.

"Dreams seldom have *any* rules," he insisted, shifting his position in his sleep.

"So, anything can happen in a dream?" she persisted.

"Of course it can."

"Is there anything that can't happen in a dream?" she asked.

"No, there is nothing that cannot happen in a dream."

"I have something to tell you," she declared, "Anything can happen in a dream and *almost* anything can happen in life."

"No, it can't!" he scolded.

"Are you sure?"

"Of course I'm sure!" he snapped, becoming irritated.

"Life, if we ask in the right way, can be persuaded to defy its rules."

"Nonsense!"

"Truly?"

"Truly nonsense," he snarled.

"What do you like to do in your dreams?"

"I like to fly."

"Do you fly often in your dreams?"

"Often enough."

"If life could be like a dream," she asked, "What would you do in life?"

She knew the answer. She knew it for certain, but she wanted him to say it.

"I would walk," he murmured, sadly.

"You would what?" she asked, pretending not to have heard him.

"I would walk!" he bellowed, so furious at her in his dream, that his sleeping form bellowed, too.

Upstairs, in the grand house with its grand frontage, its grand garden and its grand fence, Rhona – the man's wife – was startled. She lowered the book she was reading and looked at the floor, which was the direction of his voice. She shook her head, miserably. Hearing his words broke her heart. She would do anything for him to be able to walk again. She would even give up the ability to walk, herself. She raised her book and returned to her reading, but it was distractedly and without focus.

"Why do you fly in your dreams but you do not walk in them?" Greesha asked the old man in his dream.

"Because I cannot walk when I wake up. It destroys me. It breaks me into pieces. It makes waking up a horrible thing."

"Will you walk *for me* in this dream?" she asked.

"I could make *you* burst into flames," he threatened, "I could *make you* spin up into the sky in a cloud of dust."

"Will you?"

"Don't tempt me, wee lass!"

"But surely, as you have said, anything can happen in a dream."

"Yes, anything what-so-ever," he growled, "Anything, if I *want* it to happen."

"Then, maybe, this isn't a dream we're in."

"This is definitely a dream."

"Then walk for me in this dream."

"What is the point?"

"Maybe, if I ask for you in the right way, in *exactly* the right way, and if I believe…"

"*I will never walk again in my life!*" he screamed, both within his dream and out loud.

Rhona stood up from her chair, dropped her book to the floor and ran to the top of the stairs. She could hear him, asleep on the couch in the sitting room, writhing and struggling and murmuring. She put her hand to the base of her throat and sobbed.

"Walk for me!" urged the little girl, "Walk for me in this dream."

"No! No! No! I can't walk and I don't deserve to walk!"

The little girl in his dream came close to him, placed a hand either side of his face and looked into his eyes, earnestly.

"You didn't kill your brother. He didn't die because of you."

The old man was incandescent with fury, but when she touched the tip of her finger to the middle of his forehead, he became perfectly calm again.

"Your brother died because he did not do as you told him. You made him promise. You wouldn't take him to the peak of the mountain until he swore to obey your instructions."

The old man looked heartbroken.

"Your brother promised you that he would do as he was told. What did he say?"

The old man's lips trembled as he spoke.

"My brother said: *'I promise on my word of honour'*."

"But he broke his promise, didn't he?"

"Yes."

"He fell to his death."

The man gave a jolt at these words and let out a moan before replying.

"Yes," he agreed.

"Your brother fell because he wouldn't listen to you. You fell, too, trying to save him."

The man nodded, glumly.

"You risked your life to save your brother, but you couldn't save him."

The man began to cry.

"The injury you suffered, Sir, was not to your legs. Your injury was to your mind."

"No!" he argued, "My legs stopped working."

"Your legs no longer work because of what happened inside your head."

The man shook his head, weeping, but no longer contradicted her.

"Walk for me in this dream and you will walk for me as you sleep," she demanded.

"I cannot!"

"Walk for me in this dream!" she shouted, "Walk for me, so that your sleeping body will walk in real life."

Rhona Merricroft, sensing her husband's distress, raced down the stairs, threw open the door to the room and burst in. She gave a shriek as – with his eyes firmly closed – the man she loved, suddenly sat bolt upright on the couch. When Greesha next spoke, his wife heard her voice, too.

"You did *not* let your brother down, Robert! It was *you* who were let down by *him!*"

His wife looked towards the sound of Greesha's voice. She gave another shriek as Greesha appeared out of nowhere.

"Your brother would be alive today," said Greesha, vehemently, "If he had done what you said."

The man whimpered and shook his head.

"His death was not your fault," Greesha yelled at the top of her voice.

His wife, weeping uncontrollably nearby, furiously nodded her agreement.

"His death was his own fault," Greesha shouted.

His wife nodded even harder.

"The blame is not yours and never has been," Greesha told him, her voice trembling with rage.

He shook his head.

"Walk for me, Robert!" Greesha demanded, "Stand up and walk!"

With difficulty, Robert Merricroft began to shuffle to the edge of the sofa. His wife's eyes sprang open as big as a pair of milk bucket lids.

# CHAPTER 19

Greesha – with her eyes firmly shut – spoke urgently to Robert Merricroft's son from the corner of his carriage.

"Quick! Hurry! Tell your driver that the horses must gallop! It is your father! Rush as fast as you can!"

John partially opened the door to the carriage and shouted up to the driver. In a moment, the vehicle was surging forward. The driver had not used his whip. He had merely called to the horses with urgency. The horses heard the command, but – more importantly – understood the vital importance. They put their heads down and charged as fast as they were able.

The carriage came around the final turn at such a speed that it slewed on the sand and gravel like the trailing end of a whip. It thundered through the gates, along the drive and – with both horses digging their hooves into the gravel – it slid to a dramatic halt.

John Merricroft made it from the carriage and up the steps of his mansion in scarcely five strides. Hurrying along the hallway, he dashed into the sitting room.

Shocked and stunned, he watched as his father precariously rose to his feet with all the unsteadiness of a newborn fawn. His eyes popped open as he took two or three steps and stopped. At that moment, his father turned to the companion from his dream and called to her.

"Wee lassie! Wee lassie!" he exclaimed, "See! Look! It is just as you said! I am walking!"

His wife, Rhona, ran to him, as did his son. Together they both hugged and kissed him.

The little girl, who had been visible only seconds ago, clapping her hands and squealing with delight, was gone. She had disappeared. Thinking that this was some kind of trick, his wife ran to the curtains and looked behind them. She looked beside the grandfather clock. She looked behind the high-backed leather armchair. She looked everywhere in the room and in the hall outside it. There was no trace of her.

# CHAPTER 20

Greesha jumped down from the carriage, declining both the aid of the metal steps and the arm of the driver. Walking at a measured pace, she mounted the steps into the house, walked to the doorway of the drawing room and stood there without entering. Old Robert Merricroft saw her arrive and watched as she made a deep curtsey to all who were gathered there.

"I'm here," she said, politely.

All heads turned to her. Robert Merricroft, standing by his own effort and with great concentration, placed one foot in front of the other and walked to where Greesha stood.

"I can walk!" he said, incredulously.

"Yes," she replied with a wink, "But you cannot fly."

At this, the old man threw back his head and laughed. He laughed like he had not laughed in years. He laughed like he had not laughed since he had buried his brother. He laughed with the unbridled joy of a man rediscovering happiness.

Robert Merricroft was happy, again.

His son, John, was happy, again.

His wife, Rhona – after waiting for happiness for so long – was finally happy, again.

# CHAPTER 21

Later that day, Robert Merricroft, once he had managed to convince his wife and son that his 'new legs' were strong enough, had taken himself off to the stables. As he entered, there was a whinny of delight from his riding horse, 'High Tower', and from his coach horses, 'Starlight' and 'Moonbeam'. The other three horses also made welcoming noises.

High Tower and the pair of coach horses were in adjoining stalls and they joined together in knocking their hooves against the wooden slats, stamping their feet and thrashing their heads around, looking for all the world like they were trying to dislodge something stuck to their manes.

By the time the old man reached them, they were in a state of utter delight, snorting loudly through their noses and making what sounded almost like purring with their lips. Robert laughed at their antics and went from stall to stall stroking, patting and scratching them. Whichever animal he attended, however, the other two protested that they were being neglected.

Eventually, each having received copious attention, the horses calmed and he was able to stand with them and pet them, one by one, without provoking further competition.

"Thank you, High Tower," he told his horse, "I apologise for not having ridden you for so long. I have neglected you sorely. Thank you for not resenting me. Thank you for having a big heart."

The horse fluttered its lips and wagged its head, seeming to have taken his meaning.

"Thank you," he told Starlight and Moonbeam, "Thank you for getting my boy to me in time to see me walk. I know you hurried and pushed hard – very hard – and I am grateful."

The two horses nodded, almost as if they understood, and looked at him adoringly.

Robert thought for a little while and, then, speaking directly to the coach horses, he began to put together an apology.

"I hope that, in the haste to get here, Ballum didn't… you know…"

Somebody in the doorway of the stable loudly cleared his throat. Robert turned to see his groom and coach driver, Ballum, stood there.

"I didn't whip them, if that's how you think they reached you at such speed."

"You didn't?"

"No, I didn't. The truth is that I hardly ever have to so much as raise the whip, never mind apply it to them. They felt not so much as a single stroke to get them here as quick. I told them to go at it with a vigour and, heeding my words, they flew along as if the Devil in person were on their tail!"

The two horses in question, straightening themselves and standing tall, appeared to swell with pride at this praise and looked at Robert Merricroft, expectantly.

"You are wonderful, wonderful animals!" he told the pair, while nodding his apology to Ballum, "You are such fine and splendid beasts!"

The pair shuffled and skittered their hooves and snorted their delight.

"You, too, High Tower," he told the third horse, who was looking a little left out, "You are a magnificent creature, too!"

High Tower shrugged and huffed, as if embarrassed by his praise.

"In my humble opinion," said Greesha, who had appeared by his side, much to the confusion of Ballum, "Those who are kind to animals are by far the most deserving of kindness themselves and most loved by the gods."

"I believe the same," replied the old man, "And I always have."

Ballum, still unsure how she could have slipped past him, agreed: "They are, indeed, words of wisdom."

# CHAPTER 22

Greesha had never been the Guest of Honour anywhere or at any time in her entire short life. She had always been an insignificant nobody to whom not a soul would pay attention. That day at Lochside Manor, she sat at the head of a large table – raised up on a large cushion – and was treated as if she were royalty.

Robert and Rhona Merricroft sat to her left and right at the nearest end of the table. Flanking them, sat their son John and the family's good friend Asif. The other dozen guests around the table were highly placed individuals from wealthy and influential backgrounds, all of whom were grateful to be invited.

Greesha found herself garbed in the most sumptuous finery, a dressmaker having been summoned to attend her to make her clothing. Only the most impressive materials had been used and it was very obvious to everyone that no expense had been spared.

Asif had been persuaded to delay his departure for yet another day and had accommodated his crew at an inn by the river. The crew were overjoyed to be spending the night in actual beds, rather than in swaying hammocks. To add to their joy, the elder Merricroft had not only arranged them a banquet of their own to celebrate his recovery, but had provided them with an extremely generous quantity of rum. This liquid bounty had been divided up by drawing random lots, the least token winning two tots of rum and the best token, ten. The winner of the ten tots had ended up unable to make it into their bed and had settled the night on the wooden floorboards beside it.

At Lochside Manor, the diners tucked into beef, chicken, lamb and venison, all of which had been cooked to perfection by the chef and her assistant cooks in the well equipped kitchens located in the basement.

The meal progressed through its various courses – each of which was more impressive than the last – leaving Greesha astonished at the lavishness of it all.

Ultimately, they reached the sweet course at the end, which had instantly become her favourite. Everyone stood up from their chairs and milled around, bearing large, shallow dishes, which they proceeded to load with items selected from a fine array of buns, cakes and pastries.

Greesha spoke politely to this person and that, indulging in whatever conversation she could manage without attracting attention to herself for her precocious way of speaking.

It was clear that nobody knew exactly what manner of healing she had performed. They did, however, know that she had played a major part in Robert Merricroft's recovery. None had even the vaguest idea that she had intruded into his dreams, so she presented herself simply as an inspiration to the patient's sudden transformation.

When the event had eventually concluded and the guests had all departed, Robert Merricroft directed her, along with Asif, into an elegant lounge room. There, he joined them, accompanied by his wife and son.

"Your situation has been explained to me by John," he told Greesha, nodding towards his son, "And it would appear that you have not only fulfilled, but excelled, your post in this household to the point of making yourself redundant."

"Even before she arrived, by your account of things, father."

"Yes, indeed," he laughed.

Rhona gave him a wistful look.

"What is it?" he asked.

"You are laughing," she replied.

"Yes. I am. Can I not laugh?"

"Of course you may! You can laugh to the point of exhaustion," she smiled, "It is just that I have not heard you laugh for these past few years."

"Well," he promised, taking her hands in his own, "I will do plenty of laughing from now on."

This delighted everyone.

"I will hold you to that promise, my dearest husband."

"I will make a point of keeping it and then exceeding it, beloved wife."

The two embraced.

"My laughing," he continued, "Is entirely thanks to this young lady."

Greesha bowed her head, her cheeks burning from being the focus of attention.

"She may stay here for as long as she wishes, as our honoured guest, and need not expend one jot of effort or undertake one single chore for the whole time."

Greesha got up from her seat and curtsied.

"Kind sir and most gracious madam," she replied, "There is but one thing that I would ask of you, as a kindness, if you would be agreeable?"

"Ask it and it shall be done."

"It may not please you."

"Ask me, anyway, and do not worry."

"I do not want you to think me ungrateful."

"I'm sure I won't but, in that case, ask me without delay."

"First, can I enquire, please: Who made the statue that stands in the alcove, over there, by the tall clock and the bookcase?"

All eyes turned to the statue. Greesha had felt her gaze being drawn to it the moment she had entered the room.

"That statue is one of my favourite pieces of art in this house," he declared, "It is the work of a sculptor who lives in Iudeu in Pictland. He is very gifted. I would like to buy more of his things before too long."

"Your son gave me my freedom. It was a very kind and generous thing to do. I would like to ask, please, if it could be revoked and if I could be sold as a slave to the man who made the statue?"

"You wish to leave us, already?"

"Sir, I have a calling to do things. It is a calling that I cannot resist. I feel that I have work I must accomplish. I know that it sounds completely ridiculous for someone of my age to say such a thing, but I swear to you that it is the truth."

Robert Merricroft looked at her sadly.

"I was hoping that you would grow up here and that you would be part of our household, but if you want to leave…"

"Sir, it is not that I am *wanting* to leave. It is that I *must* leave. If I do not go and do the things that I know I must, then things in the future that must happen will not happen."

Hearing her careful choice of words, her host's head spun round and she found a piercing look meeting her eyes.

"Is this just one thing that must happen," he asked, "Or is it many things?"

"I choose my words with caution, Sir, for I would not wish them to be taken for disloyalty or treachery."

"I have little to do with the clans, so their doings are no concern of mine. The Vikings, however, are another matter. They have come here to Glasgow in peace, but I know that others amongst their number have brought death and destruction to areas in the north."

"Those other Vikings," his son cursed, "Are a plague of fire and death."

So saying, he made the motion of spitting, but without actually doing it, inferring that their name left a foul taste in his mouth.

"They have desecrated monasteries and abbeys," his mother responded, "And murdered priests and monks."

Robert Merricroft nodded, gravely, before responding.

"If you are not loyal to those people, little girl," he declared, "Then your loyalty is perfectly fine with me, no matter who it might involve."

"My loyalty is to one who *is* and to one who *will* be."

The elder Merricroft narrowed his eyes at her.

"You are a seer?" he asked, immediately looking to his son, John, and their friend Asif for confirmation.

They both raised their palms and shrugged their shoulders with expressions of comic confusion.

"It wouldn't surprise me," said one.

"Her talents know no limits," said the other.

"I see things that have not yet happened," Greesha volunteered.

"And where is it that you see yourself, if not here?" asked Robert, adopting a more kindly tone.

"With your permission and your assistance, Sir, I would see myself serving the household of that sculptor."

"But I can offer you a life of privilege and luxury, here."

"That is very kind of you, Sir, but I have lived a life a poverty, so privilege and luxury is a foreign land to me."

"A land that you are very welcome to inhabit."

"I must prepare the way for things that will happen in the future of Alba."

"I live in Glasgow. Why should I worry about them and their country?"

"For it will, one day, Sir, become your people's country, too."

"Why? How?"

"Glasgow in the Kingdom of Strathclyde and Edinburgh in the Kingdom of Northumbria will, one day, both be part of a new country called 'Scotland'. It will stretch from the very most northern tip of Alba to a new border a long way towards the south."

"How far south?"

"The new country of Scotland will reach all the way to the fortress town of Carlysle on one coast and to Berwick on the bank of the River Tweed on the other."

"That is a huge country."

"Yes, indeed."

"A country with one king or queen to rule it?"

Greesha looked a little embarrassed and creased her brows before replying.

"The Scottish Monarchs will claim sovereignty over the whole of Scotland."

Robert looked at her curiously.

"You have used around a dozen words in your answer, when you could have simply said 'Yes' or "No', could you not?" he probed.

She squirmed, her discomfort obvious.

"Unless," he suggested, "A 'Yes' would have been a lie."

"Not a lie…"

"But not the truth?" he suggested.

"Not the *whole* truth."

"You can see the future?"

"I can see things that will be and I can see things that will very likely be."

"I have a life, now, that is worth living," said Robert Merricroft, "It is a life that I will embrace and celebrate, but – in recent times – I have wondered about..."

He fell silent, not managing to muster quite the words that he wanted. Greesha reached and touched his arm in a most grown up gesture.

"You have begun to wonder about the future of your line."

"Yes," he said, surprised.

"You need not think that your existence has been for no good purpose," she assured him, "You need not worry that you have no real achievements that will mark out the future. Of your line, through your son and through generations of sons and daughters beyond them, will come a man of greatness, a trader who will sail the seas, explore new lands, find new cultures, and worry – just as you – that there might be more to his life than he is yet to find."

"Tell me more."

"He will be a man famous for his charity and generosity. By the example of his deeds, his own son will shape the future of Scotland. He will be a Duke and, when his time of test arrives, he will stand up to the mark and will reach way beyond it. All the lives that come before him will be worthwhile and meaningful because they will have led to his life, which he will so well and bravely live."

"You say that, of my line, will come a man famous for his charity and generosity?"

"Yes."

"That would be a life well lived, indeed."

"A life that would fill you with envy."

"Why do you say so?"

"Is it not the truth?"

"It is not something I speak about."

"You are a good man with a good heart, but you are weighed down by guilt. You regarded becoming lame as a punishment but, now, being well again, you have a wish to do something in particular, but you hold back because you do not wish to let down your wife."

"When I was a boy," Robert Merricroft announced, "I did not rejoice that my father had money. I was aware that, as I grew up, mine was an existence not altogether usual. I cannot remember how old I was when I realised that I could eat when, as often and however much I liked and that those I passed in the street could not."

His wife looked at him curiously, as though this were a new person she were encountering.

"I saw hungry faces and people with empty bellies all around me and, in some childishly simplistic way, I decided that it was wrong. I questioned my father about it and he was openly hostile to my querying our situation."

"But it did not stop you."

"No, it did not. When I dared to openly compare our life of plenty with that of the poor, he was absolutely furious and told me that it was the way of life and that is had always been so since the beginning of time. Despite the strictness and severity of my father, I never doubted that he loved me. He never hugged me, he never stroked my cheek and he never said a single word of affection to me, but I always knew that he loved me."

He paused for a long moment, snatched from the room by his thoughts, before abruptly returning and continuing as if he had merely drawn a breath.

"Eventually, I grew to an age where I felt that I must act to aid those who struggled and starved."

"And your father?"

"I lived in complete and utter dread of my father finding me out. I recall having a knot in my stomach so tight, at times, that I would be doubled up because of the pain from it."

He sighed and looked into the far distance for a long moment.

"One day, I was sneaking away food, blankets and clothing to give to the poor. I was in the middle of moving my store, little by little, out of the shed behind the stables and across the field to my straw hideout by the edge of the lane. I came back to my stash and found my father's best scarf, hat and gloves atop my pile of things. I almost died of fright. I sniffed and I could smell the smoke from my father's pipe. He had been there."

He stood rigid, obviously reliving a terrifying moment.

"I was dazed and confused and didn't know what to do. I had been discovered! I was panic stricken as I contemplated the consequences for me when, before long, my father confronted me with my misdeeds. Then, my eyes fell upon several folded handkerchiefs in a neat pile. Each of them was tied with a very particular and complicated knot, favoured by my father, that unmistakably identified him. I parted the cotton fabric and peeked into one of them. I found squares of oat and raisin biscuits. I put the package to my nose and inhaled. The smell was divine! They were unmistakably the biscuits that my father would make on the back of a shovel over a camp fire when we camped in the hills. They were still warm."

Robert looked around, inviting his listeners to share his awe. They did.

"My relationship with my father was less like that of a son and his parent than that of a lowly soldier and a commanding officer in the army. That or the relationship between the humblest of servants and the Laird of the House. Our ventures out into the hills and glens, every month through Spring and Summer, were the only times that he was even remotely human with me. He would teach me how to fire a bow, how to maintain and shoot a pistol, how to gut a deer or a hog and how to carve wood. I mastered all the skills he imparted, to the point of excellence, bar that single one. I found it difficult to carve and had no knack for it. As I failed to grow in competence, however, I revelled in my disappointing him in that one thing."

Robert's audience nodded in appreciation.

"My father always said that a blade imparted the unique signature of the carver to a piece of wood. When I was not wilfully trying to disappoint my father, I practiced carving by myself a lot. Soon, I became quite skilled at it. After learning that my father was aware of my charitable endeavours and that he had deliberately chosen not to intervene, I spent the whole of that night carving a deer for him, effectively giving up the only thing I had withheld. I left it on the handle of the door to my father's study. On the inside of its rear leg, I had inscribed in tiny little characters the words: *'My father is the very best'*. In those days, I spent a long time away from home at one or other of the local monasteries, being educated by the monks, but my mother told me that he treasured that deer more than anything else in his life."

"Why did you never tell me this story?" asked Robert Merricroft's wife.

"I have lived my life in the way I thought I was born to live it," he replied, "And have hardly ever called to mind much of my younger days, let alone spoken of them. I grew up, I joined the army, I became an officer and, then, I eventually left and, ultimately, took over my father's business."

"But now the younger version of you calls to the older you?"

"Yes, I suppose it does."

"I, too, was born into a wealthy family," said Rhona, as if it were a confession of a dark secret, "And I knew, even from the youngest age, that I had a life that was above and beyond that of ordinary people."

Robert Merricroft looked at his wife as if he were seeing a new version of her.

"I married you, my husband, despite you having attained your fortune and – very much indeed – not in any way *because* of it. If anything, your wealth was an impediment to me marrying you. I thought long and hard about it before consenting to be your wife. I felt that I had lived a life of privilege for much too long, already."

"I did not know that you felt that way."

"No. Perhaps I should have told you. I held back and acted out the role I thought I was meant to fulfil in society."

"It seems like we both, somehow, lost ourselves."

"I may have lost myself, Dearest Husband, but I also found myself in you."

"As did I, too, in you."

"I would not have wished to be with any other man."

"Nor I with any other woman."

"But, now, what we had kept buried has rushed to the surface."

"Yes," he replied, joining Rhona in looking directly at Greesha, "I wonder by what cause?"

Greesha smiled and shrugged her shoulders.

"I thought you might both wish to live the best of your lives for the rest of your lives."

"This is your doing?" asked Robert.

"Another one of your miracles?" asked Rhona.

"Sometimes life calls to us in a whisper," Greesha advised, "Sometimes it shouts to us."

"I hear it shouting!" laughed Rhona, "At the top of its voice."

"It is deafening me!" laughed Robert, covering his ears.

Greesha turned to the younger Merricroft.

"John?" she asked.

"Whatever my father and my mother wish to do will have my full support."

His parents both thanked him and hugged him.

"I can run the business on your behalf," their son explained, "And give you both your proper share of the money it makes."

"And your father and I, for our part," suggested his mother, "Can spend our remaining years on this Earth endeavouring to lessen the suffering of the poor."

"In any possible way that we can," confirmed her husband.

"The best of our lives…" whispered Rhona.

"For the rest of our lives," replied her husband.

# CHAPTER 23

Asif stepped aboard his boat with great reluctance, tears brimming in his eyes. Greesha, along with John, Robert and Rhona, called their farewells for as long as there was any chance of them being heard. Then, they waved and waved until Asif's boat was just a dot in the distance. Greesha's waving was with such enthusiasm that her companions feared she might fall into the water and had to take a grip of her to prevent it.

Asif had accepted Greesha's assurances about his journey at face value. She had promised him that his return to Morocco would not be any later as a result of his delayed departure. He had noted her words and not questioned the truth of them for a moment.

As his vessel sailed down the Irish coast, the sea became as calm as the water on a lake. Scarcely a wave could be seen and his sailors were unable to stop themselves from coming to the rails and peering over the side, at regular intervals, to reassure themselves that it was not an illusion.

The seas were remarkably calm all the way to the coast of Portugal and all aboard agreed that the time they had lost by staying over in Glasgow had been more than compensated by these truly miraculous sea conditions.

# CHAPTER 24

The drive back to Lochside Manor from the jetty was a joyous one. A new life lay ahead of all parties and they were confident that the choices they had made were the right ones.

John Merricroft was to become the manager of the family business with immediate effect, moving out of his rooms on the uppermost floor of the building into a plush master suite on the first floor.

John's parents were leaving Lochside Manor to set up a refuge for orphaned and abandoned children where they would move on with their lives to become teachers.

Greesha was moving on, too, leaving Glasgow for Iudeu, a town which, one day, would be called 'Stirling'.

Robert Merricroft refused to simply write a letter of recommendation for Greesha. Nor would he settle for despatching her in a simple covered wagon with a servant and a guard on horseback. Instead, he insisted on accompanying her, in person, and taking her in his own coach.

The journey was brief and uneventful, but – to the delight of both – it was filled with wonderful conversation.

When they drew up in front of Greesha's new home and she climbed down out of the coach, even the horses seemed disappointed to see her go. They nuzzled her, snuffled her and whinnied to her at length and looked forlorn as she finally walked away and into the sculptor's house. Robert went inside with her, making a fuss of her, himself.

A servant greeted them and, on learning their identity, disappeared to carry word of their arrival.

"We will find him in bed," Greesha whispered, shielding her mouth with her hand.

"It is most of the way to Noon," Robert replied, dubiously, "So I hardly think so."

"We will find him in bed," She repeated.

"And why so?"

"He is ill. He has a fever."

"I won't ask you how you know."

Greesha smiled in return and he squeezed her arm, affectionately. A minute later, the sculptor's wife appeared, looking slightly flustered.

"Robert," she greeted, "It is good to see you."

"And you, too."

"I wish these were better circumstances," she apologised, "For my husband will be sad to have missed you."

"Missed me?"

"Yes," she explained, "He…"

"Has a fever," Greesha interrupted.

The sculptor's wife looked alarmed and shot Greesha a look of undisguised hostility.

"Who is she? What is she?" the woman demanded of Robert, gritting her teeth and looking vexed.

"I will need fresh mint leaves from your garden," Greesha told her, not waiting for any explanation to be given, "And ginger root, liquorice root and aniseed."

"We don't have such a thing as aniseed," snapped the woman.

"It's in the jar with the head of a snake on the lid."

"We don't have any jars with the head of a snake!"

At this, a nearby slave cleared their throat, tentatively, before speaking in a faltering, timid voice.

"The master has such a jar, on a high shelf in the upper room, beneath the eaves."

The sculptor's wife whirled on them, "Fetch it then," she growled, "Or do I need to lay a cane on your back to get you moving?"

The slave rushed away, to set about the task, visibly trembling. It was clear that the threat of violence had not been an idle one. The sculptor's wife looked after the slave through narrowed eyes. Once they were out of the room, she turned back. Seeing that Greesha's eyes had come to rest on her withered arm, she barked with renewed fury.

"Look away!" she spat, "How dare you look at me so without my permission?"

Robert looked perplexed.

"What kind of slave is this?" the woman protested, "To stare at people without a jot of modesty about her."

"If you lived closer to Glasgow," Robert replied, testily, "You might know what kind of person she is, for you would have had Dinner with me last night, and – so that it is fully understood – she is no slave. She is a free woman."

"Woman!" she spluttered, "*Woman*, you say?"

Robert laughed loudly, which only served to add to her anger.

"Woman. Girl," he chuckled, "Whatever she might be. I do declare, Marie, that it is hard to tell from one moment to the next!"

The woman blinked at him, utterly baffled, but his use of her name appeared to take much of the sting from her wrath. When she rounded on a second slave in the room, she very nearly spoke to them like they were a human being.

"What are you doing still here?" she called to the other slave, "Why are you not in the garden gathering the other ingredients?"

The slave ran out of the door.

"Slaves. Servants," she complained, "People who work with their hands, all worthy of nothing but contempt."

Greesha lifted her chin, defiantly, and Marie turned to her, with her eyebrows raised.

"Your husband was once a carpenter," she said, mildly.

Marie smiled, for the first time, and her entire features promptly changed, becoming instantly pleasant and cordial.

"Why, so he was," she said, nostalgically, and – in an instant – shedding every scrap of ire.

"A noble skill. A fine talent," Greesha declared.

"Happy days," she replied.

"Until you were afflicted?"

The woman looked down at her arm and grimaced.

"A punishment from the gods."

"No. An illness you suffered. A malady that found you. It was no punishment."

"How do you know?" she demanded, sullenly.

Greesha ignored her and walked over to the fireplace. On top of it was arranged a line of fine porcelain figures. Some were people on foot, some were mounted on horseback, one was being carried in a chair with shafts attached to it. Greesha admired them at length, before turning back to address the lady of the house.

"Sometimes – when something happens for no proper reason that they can grasp – people try to explain it in whatever way they can. They need, somehow, to make sense of it."

Marie pursed her lips into a thin line, but did not reply.

"Tell me, if you will my lady," asked Greesha picking up one of the little statues, "Which of these is your favourite piece?"

The woman jolted and took half a step forward, raising her good hand in either a threat or a warning.

"Put that down!" she hissed, "Do not touch them! Leave them alone this instant!"

Greesha placed it back on the mantle shelf, but defiantly picked up another one, instinctively knowing it to be her favourite, and tossed it up and down on the cupped palm of her hand.

"Stop! Stop!" howled the woman, in genuine alarm, "If you damage that I will have you killed."

Greesha smiled, sweetly, but continued to toy with the item, causing the woman to become frantic.

"I warn you!" she threatened, "I will have you killed! I swear it! If you damage that it any way, you will pay for it with your life!"

Greesha held out the delicate little figure at the end of an outstretched arm, then suspended it, there, between finger and thumb.

"Stop!" the woman screamed at the brink of panic.

Greesha smiled her sweetest and most enchanting smile, before drawing the statue back in her arm and throwing it to the woman across the room.

The woman screamed and – stepping forward to catch it – managed to snatch it from the air.

"You dare to defy me?" she cursed, "I will have your head cut from your shoulders!"

The woman cupped the tiny figure to her breast and gave a sob, then held it before her, relishing its safety, and gazed at it, adoringly.

Robert Merricroft gawped at her. Greesha beamed at her. The woman looked from one to the other, utterly confused, having completely failed to register what had actually just happened.

"What?" she demanded.

Robert Merricroft's eyes goggled as he looked at her.

"What?" Marie asked, again, now plaintively.

"Your hand," he replied.

She looked down at the hand in which she held the statue and screamed. The two slaves – that very moment returning from their respective missions – jumped in alarm and stared in disbelief at their owner.

"Your arm!" cried one, staring open-mouthed.

"It is well!" cried the other, adopting the same expression.

"It is a miracle!" gasped Marie MacKenzie.

"It truly is," Robert confirmed in awe.

"*You* have done this!" she squealed, looking at Greesha with sudden adoration.

"No, I have not," replied Greesha, holding up her hands, defensively, "No more than an arrow shot by an archer is responsible for flying through the air and hitting its target."

"You *made* this happen!"

"I am just the arrow," Greesha pleaded.

"Then who is the archer?"

"There is a power sent into this world by the force that made it and everything that came before it," Greesha responded, "It is a power that is beyond our understanding and one that is more potent and more terrible than anything we can ever imagine."

The woman, now with two good arms and two good hands, fell to her knees.

"The gods be praised!" she sobbed.

"The power that I describe came before the gods and will last beyond the gods," Greesha insisted.

"Praise be to whatever has cured me!"

"Praise be to the force," Greesha agreed, "And praise be to the power that created it."

"Name anything you wish, anything that I can give, and it will be yours!" Marie beseeched.

Greesha looked at the woman and smiled at her.

"I woke up this morning," said Greesha, "And I could see. I could hear. I could speak. I could stand. I could walk. These gifts are all given to me without my asking. They are a constant blessing. I give thanks for them by passing on my good fortune, in any way that I can, to other people."

"You want nothing?"

"I am blessed manyfold, already, and I am free and at liberty."

"Then, in your name, I will free my slaves," the woman cried, "I will give them both their liberty."

The two slaves – now, abruptly, former slaves – slapped a hand to their chest in surprise.

"Not only that," Marie went on, "But I will pay them for the work they have done for me since I have owned them and I will pay them, from now on, a fair wage if they are willing to stay with me."

The two slaves exchanged looks of joy, but – after a few seconds – these became tinged with a little caution. Marie MacKenzie looked at the ground, suddenly ashamed.

"And I will treat them kindly," came her further declaration, "And never beat or threaten them ever again."

The two slaves, visibly relieved, hugged each other, smiling and weeping with happiness.

"Little girl, can you ask too, please, that my husband be likewise cured and restored to health?" Marie asked, with tears streaming down her cheeks, "I will take back my withered arm, if only he can be well, again."

"You would be willing to do that, My Lady?"

"I would, without a moment's hesitation."

"You say this truly?"

"Yes, truly."

Greesha gave her a bleak and forlorn smile, impressed by her selflessness. Then, she closed her eyes and hoped and prayed. She willed that the thing the woman had wished, would be so. Within a moment, the woman's arm was once again dangling by her side, completely useless. Marie MacKenzie looked down at her limb and, with no regret, gave a cry of joy.

"Thank you! Thank you! Thank you!" she said.

"Your husband's fever is gone. He  is cured."

"You have my eternal gratitude."

"You have no regret?" asked Greesha.

"No, none what so ever."

"You said that you could not imagine the goodness, the kindness and the love of the world beyond this world?"

"Yes, I did."

"You do not need to imagine it, My Lady, for you have demonstrated it, this very moment."

"This arm of mine is merely a blackened, gnarled and crooked limb that has been this way for ten years. My husband loves me no less for it. He is my whole world. I love him more than life itself."

With those words, she ran to the door and could be heard running up the stairs, calling her husband's name.

"It is sad," said Robert, "That her arm had to be made wizened, again."

"It is a bargain she freely chose," Greesha explained, "And the truth of her devotion needed to be tested."

Robert looked crestfallen, "But you said that she had demonstrated the love of the world beyond this world."

"Yes, she has, and – for that reason – the return of her ailment will be only temporary."

Robert looked hugely relieved.

Upstairs, the woman's husband had awoken. Previously too frail and weak to speak in more than a whisper, he shouted a reply to his wife in a clear, strong voice. She yelped with joy and ran still faster, up the last of the steps and into the bedroom.

"Stop!" shouted Greesha, so loudly that her voice rang through the whole house.

The footsteps above her halted. Greesha closed her eyes and drew in the spark of inspiration she had felt, before, and let it blossom. There was a shriek through the floorboards above her head, followed by a man's voice.

"Your arm!" her husband exclaimed in astonishment, "Your arm is well, again!"

"Your love has cured you both," said Greesha, her voice nothing more than a whisper, but heard with crystal clarity by both of the people upstairs.

Robert Merricroft put an arm around Greesha and pulled her close to him.

"It is surely a fact," he said, solemnly, "That all of the very best stories have a happy ending."

# CHAPTER 25

Balgair McRory could hardly believe his eyes.

Balgair McRory could hardly believe his ears.

Balgair McRory could hardly believe he was awake.

As he neared his village, the people on the road had become more and more numerous. At first, he thought that they might be going to some unrelated gathering and that he had encountered them by chance. Before long, however, he had come to the unavoidable conclusion that they were there to celebrate his return.

The men who had been his original escort, had already been paid for their services when they had been hired. This, Balgair knew, could only mean that their integrity was beyond question. Such was the buoyant mood of The MacDonald, however, that he pressed additional money onto them and, despite their protests, would not hear of them declining it. Whatever might be about to happen, Balgair deduced, the honour of playing any part in it was something that went far beyond mere money.

Balgair's new escort was comprised of riders of his own Clan and of neighbouring Clans and they had a similar attitude. They all rode tall in the saddle with their heads held high, relishing their task and proud to be selected.

The closer they came to their destination, the more Balgair found himself becoming nervous. As they crested the last hill and began the shallow descent to the broad meadow where his village lay, there were flags and ribbons hanging from tall poles driven into the ground by the road.

One of the riders, whom Balgair recognised as a relative, leaned closer to him from his saddle and declared: "The hero returns!"

Balgair would recall, for the rest of his life, his witless and feather-brained reply, which was: "Who is the hero?"

It wasn't long before his riding companions began to disperse, heading off the track and across the grass to take up positions in a wide perimeter. This, he realised, must be the gathering point.

From the far yonder, up the road, Balgair noticed a horse galloping towards him. It was raising a dust cloud in its wake. The horse moved with such powerful grace that it seemed to be carried by the wind. The person on its back appeared less *upon* the horse as they did a *part* of it. He felt a thrill to witness their approach and a pang of envy for whoever could ride a horse, such as that, in such an impressive manner.

The horse arrived in an almost impossibly rapid time and the rider leapt from the saddle in a fluid, elegant movement like a dancer. Balgair was left gaping in awe. The rider removed their dust mask, shook their head from their hood and let a cascade of long, dark, gold flecked hair fall about their shoulders like a wave of chestnut silk. Balgair's eyes widened as he realised that the rider was a woman.

"Sir, I come to give you my thanks," she said, both bowing and crooking a leg like an abbreviated curtsey, "They are thanks that are long overdue."

"I just saw you bow," he blabbered, cursing himself for the stupidity of the remark and cursing his tongue for tangling his words.

"Would you have me crouch and hold out my skirts like some frail and feeble creature?"

"No, I..."

"I am not the same timid girl on whose behalf you once intervened. You should see me fight with a sword, an axe or a spear."

"I expect you to behave as you would wish and to be true to yourself."

She blinked for a moment, in surprise at his reply, then smiled a dazzling smile.

"You are she?" he asked, dismounting from his saddle with an athletic move that scarcely matched hers.

He grimaced at his landing but, charitably, she raised an eyebrow and made a slight inclination of her head to signify her approval of his feat. He felt gratified and decided that he liked her very much.

"Sir, if it were not for your intervention, I would very likely be dead."

At that precise moment a strand of ribbon, lofted by a breeze, wafted across in front of her. In a lightning fast move, she drew out a half-sword, and – with a back and forth motion – sliced the ribbon three times before it fell, limply, to the ground.

"If there were a rematch," he proclaimed, "Their guts would be laying around your feet in a lake of blood."

"Those men are no more," she replied, "You slew two of them and mortally wounded the third."

"And the fourth man?"

"He was the one who held me around my neck. My father's dogs took his scent from my clothing and tore him to pieces when they caught him."

"I am lucky he did not set those hounds upon me."

"My father loves his hounds," she laughed, "And would not have risked their teeth or claws by setting them about a lowly horse thief."

Balgair opened his mouth to deny the charge, but she raised a hand and gave him her beautiful smile.

"You were a fleeing man who stopped to risk his life and, at the very least, the chance of a wound that might slow him down and get him caught."

"It was not a noble act."

"You saw nothing of my face," she scoffed, "And little if anything of my hair and only a hint, at best, of…" she hesitated, "My shape."

She stood up tall and he found himself immediately impressed by her physique. Finding himself staring, he quickly averted his eyes.

"I meant it was instinct," he spluttered, "Any actual decisions were overwhelmed by my training and my sense of chivalry."

Heather MacDonald promptly lowered her head, hunched down and raised her arms, as if to shield herself, visibly cringing with embarrassment at her brief flash of arrogance.

"However," he hurriedly declared, "One second longer and your appearance would have had me completely enthralled!"

She brought a hand to her face to hide any potential blush and slowly recovered her composure before forcing herself to raise her head and look at him. Balgair, she observed, had his eyes cast to the ground, studiously ignoring her moment of fluster. It was a kindness for which she found herself grateful, accepting that he would have been within his rights to have sneered at her for her little outburst of vanity.

"You can look at me," she whispered.

"I don't want to make you feel awkward."

"You're far too kind."

"You're entitled to feel proud of yourself for how you look." He replied.

"I'm vain and immodest."

"No."

"I remain more of an impetuous girl than a grown woman."

"You're being too harsh."

"I think not."

"I am sure it is so."

As he raised his gaze, she smiled a radiant smile.

"Whatever woman is in your life, she is most fortunate."

"There is no such woman."

Heather knotted her brows.

"How so?"

"I fell in love with a girl when I was young. My admiration for her was at a distance. She always had her friends around her and I was too shy approach her. We exchanged many long glances and lingering looks, but I never mustered the courage to tell her how I felt. Then she left. Her father was called away to serve a Laird in the north. I have never seen her again. Now, I find myself somehow tethered to her memory."

"That is some confession."

Balgair frowned, unsure if he were being mocked. Before he could reach a conclusion, he found she had pressed a finger against his lips to quieten him.

"Sir, I do not taunt or deride you."

Suddenly, they both heard the noise of hooves and realised, simultaneously, that a rider had approached close to them while they had been distracted. Balgair saw a look of horror sweep across her face as it dawned on her that her finger was still firmly on his lips and clearly visible to the rider.

"Oh, my word!" chortled the newcomer, "To what secret has she bound you?"

Heather, immediately recognising her uncle's voice, clenched her teeth and bared them at Balgair, mimicking a skeleton's grin, to show her unease.

"It's her worst possible secret, I'm sorry to say!" Balgair laughed, hoping that his impulse to say this might pay off.

"What? That she is betrothed to an Englishman you mean?" came her uncle's reply.

Heather laughed at length, mostly spurred by relief, and gave Balgair a look of gratitude.

"Oh! The shame!" cried Balgair, now bursting into genuine laughter.

"Let a pack of devils take the both of you!" she sniggered, whirling around to glare at her uncle.

"She has brought disrepute on our clan!" her uncle announced, grinning broadly.

"You must find yourself heckled and jeered throughout Scotland!" Balgair replied.

"I'll tie you both in sacks and drown you in the brook!" Heather chortled, striking Balgair's shoulder with her fist as if they were good friends.

Her uncle climbed from his saddle and, taking Balgair's hand, shook it fervently.

"Our family owes you her life," he said.

"It was my privilege to have been there at the right moment, but – in truth – I had mistaken her for a stranger," Balgair confided, crossing his fingers behind his back to neutralise the deceit.

The man gave him a look that had a tinge of curiosity about it.

"I did not recognise her until later," Balgair lied, with a casualness he found disturbing, "When I recalled all the times, as children, that she and I had beaten the bracken and gorse together during the grouse hunting."

Her uncle chuckled at this entirely fictitious recollection, accepting it as explaining the casualness of how they had been standing so close together.

As the three of them moved to mount their horses, Heather and Balgair turned to steal a conspiratorial glance. For both, the baffling spontaneity of their friendship remained a mystery.

# CHAPTER 26

Word of Balgair McRory's return had spread around the local population like wildfire and a feast in his honour had been announced immediately. Everybody, it seemed, loved the idea of a man who had departed in shame but returned as a hero.

The crowds that had gathered spilled out of the village square in a procession that made its way up the road and into the meadow, cheering, chanting and singing. They were plainly overjoyed at the prospect of a celebration, especially one that was to involve drinking ale and roasting hogs over a fire pit.

In the middle of the throng, The MacDonald climbed onto the back of a wagon and held up a hand, causing the gleeful crowd to quickly hush.

"My daughter is alive and well," he declared, "Thanks to the courage of one man."

A huge cheer went up, growing louder and louder. A smile played upon the lips of The MacDonald as he bided his time until the noise had faded enough for him to continue.

Balgair cringed with embarrassment as he was hustled up onto the wagon.

"This man," The MacDonald shouted, "Was falsely accused of stealing a horse. His honour and integrity were despicably insulted."

There was another cheer from the audience and, again, the speaker patiently waited for it to subside.

"But he proved himself."

The crowd responded with another cheer and a wave of loud applause.

"He showed himself to be a man of courage."

More cheering and applause ensued.

"He showed himself to be a fine example of what it is to be a Highlander."

Again, more loud vocal approval.

"This man is Balgair McRory," proclaimed The MacDonald, lifting the hero's arm aloft, as if he were the victor in a fistfight, "And I am proud that he and his people are a part of the Clan MacDonald."

This time, the shouting, cheering, applause and stamping of feet was ecstatic and took a minute and a half to yield to quiet. The Clan Chief, happy that he had conveyed his main message, was content to allow them to settle in their own time. When, at last, they had calmed, he held up a leather purse.

"This purse contains my additional thanks," he said, "Expressed in the form of silver."

Balgair, took the purse cautiously, like he were being handed a poisonous snake. The crowd erupted into such a bout of ecstatic chanting, that The MacDonald abandoned any further attempts at announcements and simply gestured for them to begin feasting.

Once they had climbed back down to ground level, The MacDonald led Balgair a good way from the noise to make conversation easier.

"You don't like silver?" he asked.

"I have nothing against silver," Balgair assured him, "My problem is that I do not require a reward for simply doing the right thing."

"I'm insulting your honour?"

"No. It isn't anything that I can explain. I don't mean to be ungrateful."

"A man of integrity is worth a hundred men who have none."

Balgair looked his leader in the eye, having previously kept his gaze down, out of respect. The MacDonald gave him a long, shrewd look. Balgair felt he was being very carefully assessed.

"Did it not occur to you, young McRory, to simply leave my daughter to her fate?"

"No!" snapped Balgair, aghast, "It did not!"

"I thought so!"

Balgair tried to reply but, without the words, he abandoned his attempt.

"Balgair McRory, I have a mission for you if you will accept it."

"I will do anything you command."

"That's not good enough."

Balgair looked at him in confusion.

"I don't want you to simply obey my command, Balgair. This is something that requires your heart and soul to be invested in it."

"I promise…"

"Don't make me promises until you know more."

Balgair opened his mouth to reply, but then closed it.

"My daughter, Heather, in a moment of foolishness, slipped away from her escort. While they were searching for her, she was stopped by four bandits. Her life was at risk. She was in mortal peril. They were four big men and you were by yourself, but you did not hesitate. You drew your sword in a flash. She said so. You didn't stop to weigh up the situation. You acted."

Balgair looked embarrassed.

"There are certain men who cannot be bought and whose nature cannot be corrupted. They are either made of the right metal or they are not. There is no in between."

The MacDonald leaned even closer to Balgair.

"We live in dangerous times. There are things afoot that are deeply troubling. It is at moments like this that I need people whom I can trust. I know I can trust you."

"What is it you wish me to do?"

"We'll talk away from here," said The MacDonald, placing and arm around his shoulder and steering him away in the direction of a nearby group of trees, "Somewhere where we will not be overheard."

The Chieftain of the Clan MacDonald gestured to his soldiers and they arranged themselves in a circle around them, at a discrete distance.

"I need to place the future of Scotland in your hands."

His words left Balgair stunned.

"The future of Scotland?"

"The future of *our* Scotland. The future of the *true* and *righteous* Scotland."

"That is a heavy responsibility."

The MacDonald cautiously looked around, in all directions, before replying.

"There is word of a threat to the life of The Queen of the West."

"A threat from whom?"

"Need you ask?"

"From the Clan Campbell?"

"The very same."

Balgair nodded, thoughtfully.

"It was, My Chief, the Campbells who slew her mother."

"Aye. They did. In the most despicable and treacherous way. She gave them an opportunity to set aside their wicked past and to begin a new future…"

"But they betrayed her."

"They betrayed her *and* they betrayed their most solemn and sacred oath."

"They were bound to her as her Honour Guard."

"A position, young McRory, of great prestige and one that should never have been allowed them."

"You say it truly."

"Who could possibly offer her an Honour Guard, now?"

"It would be an audacious thing to do!"

"Lairds across the Highlands quake at the very idea."

"And not without reason, My Chief."

"It would be an incredibly bold thing for any Laird to do."

"It would."

"They would be accused of folly."

"They would, My Chief, because the burden would be immense."

"Not just the burden of doing it."

"How so?"

"Because it would be a magnificent gesture that would elevate her status and brazenly declare her to be Scotland's hope. This, at a time when some people are beginning to doubt and to lose their faith in the Old Ways."

Balgair stood up tall and pushed back his shoulders.

"I would be proud to be a part of such an Honour Guard."

"I don't want you to be a part of her Honour Guard," replied The MacDonald.

Balgair cringed at the stupidity of his own arrogance. He wished, with every shred of his being, that a hole would open up in the ground and swallow him. The MacDonald, seeing him slump and visibly deflate, fought to suppress a smile.

"Your elevation to the rank of lieutenant was a temporary one."

Balgair's disappointment doubled and his heart dropped into his boots. With an impulse of malicious glee, The MacDonald paused for a few moments before continuing.

"I don't want you to be a part of her Honour Guard," he repeated, "I want you to *lead* her Honour Guard, as captain."

The transformation in Balgair McRory was spectacular. He suddenly stood bolt upright, as if he had been pricked with a pin, and stared, wide-eyed, in surprise.

"Me?" he asked, clearly dazed.

"Yes. You."

"I'm… I'm…"

"You are, indeed!"

"I'm…"

"Disappointed? Outraged? Furious?"

"I'm truly lost for words."

"I have many a man who is pledged to my banner who could trill words at me like a dozen sparrows, but it is not your words that concern me. It is your deeds. You can think up your reply at your own pace and take as long as you wish about it. You can take from now until the morning, if you need to, just as long as – in honour and good faith – you can give me your hand."

Balgair shot out his hand and landed it into that of the man before him.

"Now, I need my sword," the Chieftain announced, motioning to one of his guards.

A man strode across to them bearing an impressive sword that shone and gleamed.

"This is for ceremony and for show," The MacDonald grumbled, "It is not the one that I use for fighting."

The MacDonald waved away the sword and made a sign in the air. The soldier who had brought him the sword took it away and, presently, returned with a far more modest weapon.

"Since all the Queens of the West – through history – have been modest, with no great liking for making a display of wealth and luxury, it would be better to confirm your appointment with this sword, instead."

Balgair nodded in agreement and took to one knee.

"You have knelt as who you have been. I bid you rise as who you now become. You have been an ordinary rider in my cavalry and, for an hour or so a lieutenant, but you are now Captain of the Honour Guard of Her Royal Highness Queen Annis, Queen of the West."

Balgair McRory glowed as if some inner light had been switched on.

"I am honoured and privileged," he declared, placing a hand over his heart.

"Captain, in the coming days and weeks, you might end up cursing me for this honour and privilege. You might wish it had been granted someone else."

Balgair bit his tongue and obediently said nothing.

"Your troops, captain, are selected. I am a fair judge of people – if I were not, I would never have made it even close to the age I am now – so when I say that they are all pleased for you and that not a single one of them begrudges you this elevation of rank, I mean it truly."

"Thank you."

"You're going to have to endure a banquet in your honour and, in all likelihood, be called upon to make a speech."

In reply Balgair pulled a face. The MacDonald laughed.

"You and your men, captain, should fill your bellies with food and ale. Come the morning, I don't want any of you able to walk in a straight line without assistance."

Balgair grinned.

"Tomorrow," The MacDonald continued, "You and your men can spend the day being fitted for some very impressive armour. The following day, you will form up with both the members of the Honour Guard and the members of the ordinary cavalry riders who will accompany you. Not one, single man will be anything but the best that can be mustered."

Balgair nodded.

"Then, I will send you on your way. You will ride across into Inverness-shire and up to Boat of Garten. There, you will defend the queen and preserve her life."

Balgair struck his chest, three times, above his heart with his clenched fist, to confirm his obedience.

"The queen, Captain McRory, is planning to cross the River Spey and travel along the opposite bank for a distance. This is a ceremony that she performs every few years and is a traditional assertion of the boundary of her territory. My spies tell me that, this time, she is likely to face an army who oppose her. You will thwart them and vanquish whatever their plans may be."

Balgair nodded, sombrely.

"Be warned, captain, that the Clan Campbell remains hostile to the queen and it is not out of the question that you may encounter them on your travels. If you do, I want you to show them the peril that awaits them if they take up arms against the rightful Queen of the Highlands."

"Yes, My Chief."

"Her Majesty has a particular view of justice and it is far more lenient than I would ever contemplate for her enemies. Within the bounds of what she will allow, I want you to inflict the maximum possible retribution on the Campbells."

"It will be as you say."

"Do you speak English?" asked The MacDonald, abruptly switching from Scots Gaelic.

"I do," he replied, in English.

"How would you describe your familiarity with it?"

"I studied, in my youth, both in Salisbury and Winchester, south of the border, and, in those times, I used English as my primary language. I did so for at least eight years of my early life."

"I knew it, but I wished to hear you speak it."

"I am fluent."

"You are, indeed, and," he laughed, "Blessed with an English twang when you speak!"

Balgair looked mildly offended.

"I speak English like a Scotsman," he protested.

"If you do, then I am sat at the top of that mountain, over there!" he chuckled, gesturing towards the horizon.

"I'm sorry," replied Balgair, cupping a hand behind his ear and looking as if he were concentrating hard, "But I can scarcely make out a single word you're saying at that distance."

The Chieftain of The MacDonalds clapped his hands with delight, roared with laughter and slapped Balgair on his back.

# CHAPTER 27

"I want you to be very careful, little girl," said the sculptor, earnestly, "For your gifts, if exposed to too many people, could easily attract accusations of you being a witch!"

"I take what care I can, kind sir, but I sometimes feel compelled to act when it is not always entirely safe."

"If they burn you – which they will if they accuse you – there will be an end to the good deeds you perform, forever and always."

Greesha seemed to consider this advice for a few moments, before replying.

"The Vikings are coming," she announced.

"They have come, already. They have settled to the west and to the far north."

"The Vikings are coming," she repeated, "These are new Vikings. They do not wish for *part* of these lands, but for *all* of these lands."

"You say this truly?"

"I do."

"Why now, in the year 793, would the Vikings be coming, again, when they have lived here in peace in their own areas, for close to thirty years?"

"These are not the same Vikings. They are other Vikings. Vikings who have become tired of bringing death and destruction to the lands to the south of us, over the narrow sea below England, and who are seeking new conquests."

"Conquests? Is that even a word you understand?"

Greesha smiled.

"To be honest, I have lost track of what words I know and what words I do not know. I have lived for these past five, six or seven years since my birth, but I sometimes feel – in some strange way – that I have lived twenty-five years in-between them."

"Now talking like *that*," warned the sculptor's wife, Marie, "Will definitely deliver you to the fire and at a hectic speed. Your feet will scarcely touch the ground!"

"I am both who I am," Greesha reflected, philosophically, "And who I cannot possibly be."

The sculptor and his wife looked at each other, beseechingly. They still swam in an ocean of gratitude for the healing that Greesha had performed for them both and they both felt a yearning to do something for her in return. This was despite the little girl having shunned all rewards.

For whatever reason she was able, Greesha sensed exactly how they were feeling and smiled, kindly, at them.

"Would you both know me for who I actually am?" she asked.

"Yes," they replied, in unison, without a moment's hesitation.

Greesha leaned forward and was gratified when the husband and wife leaned forward, too, eager to hear her words.

"I was born on an island in the middle of the sea that lays between England, Scotland and the northern tip of Ireland."

Over the next hour, tended regularly by servants with snacks and beverages, Greesha poured forth the details of her entire existence. Her audience received her words with fascination. Greesha felt, with a mysterious certainty, that the help and good will of the couple would be an essential part of her future.

When she had finished, the sculptor leaned back in a sumptuous, padded chair and folded his arms. His wife, in an identical chair, interlocked her fingers, leaned back and placed her hands on her lap. The man looked at the woman. The woman looked at the man. The man raised his eyebrows at her. In response, the woman raised her own eyebrows, at him.

"If this is a story that you have made up," the man announced, after a long pause, "You would have to possess the most absolutely incredible imagination."

"And if it is not," the woman observed, "Then this world in which we live is a world other than we think it to be."

"Every word I have told you is true," Greesha assured them.

The couple looked at each other, nodded almost imperceptibly, and turned back to her.

"We believe you," they both said, together.

"I thank you."

"Can you tell me more of something, please?" asked Marie.

"Anything you wish."

"Tell me more about the woman you described who, you said, will oppose the Vikings and who will lead her own band of warriors against them."

"She is Kiffan. She is the first Queen of the West, that is the west of what will, one day, become Scotland. The Vikings will become impressed with her tenacity and stubbornness. They will name her 'Kiffan the Defiant'. When they choose a name for her band of soldiers, they will very much underestimate them. They will call them by a word in Norse that means *brydda* in Scots Gaelic. That word, of course, means *nuisance* in the English tongue."

Her audience nodded approvingly.

"Kiffan will eventually be captured when she is betrayed by people she will regard as allies. She will be sentenced to death by King Urokmort, leader of the Vikings, but he will not carry out that punishment because he will fear doing it. This will be because a nearby tree will burst into flames. It will burn for seven days and seven nights, but without scorching a single blade of grass around it or a single leaf or twig upon it."

Her audience was spellbound.

"To the Vikings, a burning tree is a powerful omen. It warns of great good or of great woe and doom. King Urokmort decides that he must respond to the tree on fire as a sign of good. To do otherwise, he knows, would cause fear and panic amongst his soldiers and, quite possibly, jeopardise the success of his campaign of conquest."

Her audience nodded, eagerly.

"But, the king will have already granted her the right – by virtue of her being a monarch about to be executed – to choose any reasonable act of clemency that is within his power to grant."

Her audience leaned forward in anticipation.

"She chooses that the king should grant immunity from any future attacks upon the castle where lives the man she loves."

"Your earlier shortened version of this story," objected Marie, almost indignantly, "Made no mention of any aspect of love in its telling."

"Did it not?" asked Greesha, feigning puzzlement, "Then let me go back a little way in the story."

So saying, the little girl cupped her chin in her hand and cast her eyes up to the Heavens, as if for inspiration. She paused, making a pretence of concentrating to recollect something that – in reality – she knew in the most intimate and fastidious detail. In the telling of this part of the tale, she knew, she would snare the couple's interest, engagement and concern.

"During a decisive battle against the Vikings, Kiffan and Corey Grant, the son of the Laird of Clan Grant, will both suffer life-threatening injuries. They will both be sent into the care of the monks at a monastery in the Western Isles. There, they become very close and, during their long recuperation, develop a romantic bond. The monastery grows violets in abundance in its gardens and Corey will often present bouquets of them to Kiffan. The Laird Grant is most displeased at their closeness and attempts to marry his son off to a variety of very eligible brides, but his son declines them all."

The sculptor and his wife looked intrigued.

"Later in the year, the Vikings will attack the fortified stronghouse of Clan Grant, on their way to unsuccessfully lay siege to Aberdeen. It will be Kiffan's army that rides to their rescue. With her help, they are able to hold out for the whole day, repelling charge after charge from their enemy. The Viking forces eventually leave, being summoned to join the assault on Aberdeen. The Clan Grant is saved."

Greesha's listeners beamed at this news.

"In the battle, the Laird's son – never afraid to lead his troops from the front – will be severely wounded for a second time. Still furious over his son's affection for Kiffan, his father will not allow her entry to his property and – in a disgraceful snub – she is forced to make camp outside their walls. On hearing this, his son, despite his terrible wounds, insists on being carried out to her on a stretcher. There, he presents her with a violet."

Greesha paused to allow her words to be relished.

"After days of fighting at Aberdeen, having failed to secure victory, the Vikings are driven to withdraw. The various bands of Vikings will disperse, travelling in different directions. One large group sets off back westward, retracing their original route and passing, again, the lands of the Clan Grant. Finding themselves within striking distance of the Grant Stronghouse, they decide to pay them another visit. Finding Kiffan's forces gone, the Vikings arrange themselves to begin a siege. The Laird Grant is compelled to negotiate with them and agrees to peace terms that include the regular payment of tribute."

Greesha sighed and, clasping her hands together, rested them against her chin, almost as if in prayer. There was, it appeared, far worse news to disclose.

"The Vikings will depart and head north towards home. They will follow a path that leads them to a crossroads. The Viking scouts report that there are signs that a large force has, not long ago, taken the road to the north west. Realising that this must be Kiffan and her warriors, the Vikings set off after her. They guess, correctly, that she has not gone too far, having had to travel slowly and make frequent stops due to the number of wounded in her party."

Greesha swallowed and took a deep breath before continuing.

"The Laird Grant receives a report from one of his own scouts, telling him of the situation. He musters a large rescue party. The soldiers he despatches are instructed to ride out in haste, but to stop beyond the first hill and make camp. They are to wait there and return in the morning."

Greesha's audience was shocked.

"Kiffan will not be warned of the attack by the Vikings and none of the soldiers of Clan Grant will give her assistance. The Laird Grant will leave her to be taken completely by surprise. It is not long before the Vikings find Kiffan and her troops. They fall upon them from three directions. They slay all of the wounded, on the spot, and take Kiffan prisoner."

"Disgusting!" exclaimed the sculptor.

"Disgraceful!" exclaimed his wife.

"It is, indeed, such an act of treachery that it will cause them lasting shame," Greesha announced.

"You say treachery that *will* cause them lasting shame?" asked the sculptor, "Not treachery that has *already* caused them this lasting shame?"

"Their treachery *will* definitely shame them," Greesha confirmed, evasively.

"Yes, but when does this act of treachery occur?"

"It will be in two or three years from today."

"How can you know?" asked the sculptor.

His wife gave him a look and he shrugged his shoulders and he nodded, accepting that it was a needless question.

"It is because you are *able* to know," he said.

"Yes," she agreed.

"Will the Queen of the West die?"

"I'm not able to know that."

"Why?"

"Because I shouldn't know it."

"Why?"

"Because the outcome of this tragedy will have a profound consequence on the future."

"Can you not stop it from happening?"

"No."

"Are you sure?"

"Am I sure?" Greesha laughed, "Do you think I wouldn't wish to stop it if I could?"

"Tell me," asked the sculptor, "Is it the case that, sometimes, whatever will happen will happen, no matter what you do?"

Greesha turned to him and smiled a dazzling smile.

"Very good!" she congratulated, "It takes some people a long time to reach that conclusion."

The sculptor furled a hand in the air and affected a flamboyant bow.

"My thanks," he said, grinning, "There is a lot of time to think about things when creating something from clay or stone."

"Sewing tapestries is very much the same," quipped Marie, "So, tell me little girl, if you will: Are we to believe that the future is fixed and cannot be changed?"

"Today," Greesha replied, "Is here and now in the present and – whilst we call it today – when tomorrow arrives, it will become yesterday."

The couple looked puzzled.

"If somebody throws a pebble at a bell and causes it to ring," Greesha explained, "Then preventing the bell from ringing might involve hiding the pebble to stop it from being thrown, snatching it from the air as it travels, shielding the bell from it or moving the bell out of its path."

"So we are able to change the future?" queried Marie.

"We cannot know for certain, because we cannot know which, if any, of those options might be available to us."

"So it may or may not be possible?"

"When I see the future, it is not always clear. It appears to me as being vague and imprecise, almost as often as it appears to me as distinct and precise."

"Can you say the same about the past?"

"The past is fixed. It has already gone. I don't usually have any issues seeing the past."

"So we cannot alter the past?"

"The past is what *did* happen and if anybody becomes able to alter it, then that person did, or does, alter it so that it occurs exactly the way that it has already happened."

"So the past is fixed?"

"The past is fixed unless a power that is beyond and above this world decides to intervene. In which case, the change that will happen was always going to happen, so what eventually happens to change the past is always going to be what did happen to change the past. Therefore, the past becomes what did actually happen when it was changed."

"It makes my head hurt to think about it," the sculptor declared.

"My head, too," his wife agreed.

Everyone was silent as they pondered the subject.

"So," the sculptor persisted, seeming to have encountered some kind of inspiration, "What if you went a long way into the future and, from there, changed the past that is only a short time ahead of us?"

"If ever in the future I change the past, then however things happened in the past – be it up to now or beyond now – is always going to be how I changed it."

In response, the sculptor and his wife both grasped their heads, screwed up their faces and feigned being in pain. Greesha laughed.

# CHAPTER 28

The light of the day had just started to fade when the sculptor and his wife invited Greesha to walk with them to the top of the steep bank and take in the view.

"You are probably wondering why we wanted you to come up here," said the sculptor, gesturing to the fields, the river at its far end and the mountains beyond.

"Maybe so, maybe not," replied Greesha, "For I never know what I know until the moment comes." With this, she made a puzzled face, "No," she confessed, "I *don't* know."

"This place," his wife announced, "Has a special significance for us."

Greesha gave her a wary look.

"I don't like the sound of this."

"Marie and I both make pottery. We dig the clay from the pit that sits in front of the line of trees with the bright reddish-yellow leaves. I quarry the rock for my sculptures from the foot of the mountain that rises beyond those trees."

"The clay pit," Marie explained, "Has belonged to my family for almost two hundred years."

"And the quarry bank," her husband added, "To mine for over a hundred."

Greesha looked from one to the other, conscious that they felt a need to tell her something.

"Tell me," she urged, "What is it that troubles you?"

She waited as the couple traded anxious looks.

"It won't be long, now," the sculptor assured her, "And you will know."

"I will?"

"Yes," they both insisted.

Greesha watched as the sun started to sink behind the mountains. The light began to fade rapidly.

"Something has been happening here, regularly," Marie proclaimed, "For as long as my family have been in these parts.".

"And, also," the sculptor added, "For as long as mine have, too."

"This thing of which you speak," asked Greesha, "It happens at this time of day?"

"Yes, around this time."

"Every day?"

"It happens as many days as it does not, which is for half the time."

They all stood and waited.

Greesha found something begin to stir inside her. She became aware that they were no longer alone. Somewhere, close by, she could hear the sound of feet on the ground. Not one person's feet, not the feet of several or even a small group of people, but of many, many more.

The sculptor and his wife did not need to be told that Greesha could hear the sound, for it was obvious from the expression on her face.

"Is it folly or the truth," asked the husband, "To say that a place can be haunted?"

"Haunted?" asked Greesha, mulling the word over, "Yes, when someone who has passed from this world finds themself tied to a place and cannot move on from it."

"How many people can that be?" Marie asked.

"I don't know if there is a limit."

"Could it be an entire army?"

"An entire army!" Greesha exclaimed.

"Yes."

"I suppose it could," Greesha pondered, "But that is a lot of people to find themselves bound to a single place."

"That noise," Marie exclaimed, nodding in the direction of the marching feet, "Is coming from a great number of people!"

"That is a sad and sorrowful thing to imagine," Greesha declared.

"Can it be stopped?" enquired the sculptor.

"I cannot be certain but, for their sake, I hope so."

"Listen," said Marie, holding up a finger to draw attention, "They will stop."

As if to oblige her, the marching feet abruptly ceased.

"They will wait a short while, then they will start off, again."

The feet duly stilled for a minute and then resumed their slog.

"Those are heavy feet," Greesha declared, "Weighed down by armour, by heavy weapons and by shields."

They all stood and listened as the footfalls faded away into the distance.

"They will stop, again, almost out of earshot, then start off towards the east."

They all fell silent as they strained their ears and, just as she had said, they paused and then turned eastwards.

"They are tired and weary," said Greesha, "But they are determined."

"They are soldiers," the sculptor noted, "Soldiers obeying orders."

"Do you ever see them?" asked Greesha, suddenly intrigued.

"No."

"Never?"

"Never. We hear them, but we never see them."

Greesha closed her eyes, crouched down on her haunches and put her hands either side of her head. As she did so, the army turned and began marching back towards them.

"They are lost!" cried Greesha, a wave of insight flooding her senses, "Back in their time, there is a great battle nearby and they are on their way to join it."

She stood up and held a finger aloft to emphasise her further revelations.

"They are needed, urgently. The directions they have been following, however, are wrong. The map they have is the wrong one. It shows three mountains and not two and the fork in the river they are seeking is not there."

"Who are they?" beseeched the sculptor's wife.

"They are Romans. They are part of a Roman Legion. They have been held back in reserve. They have then been summoned, and told to hurry, but they cannot find their way."

"So, now, they are reliving their torment and distress, over and over," said Marie, sadly.

"A nightmare that never ends," agreed her husband.

Greesha climbed onto a rock and stood her tallest.

"I can see them," she announced, "But they cannot see me."

"How do you know?"

"I wish I could know how I know!" Greesha laughed.

They all listened as the marching continued, then Greesha jumped down from the rock and beckoned them to follow her to a shallow mound, nearby.

"Take my hands," she urged, "And you will be able to see them. I know it."

They joined her and did as instructed and both marvelled at the sight.

"Hugely impressive," remarked the sculptor.

"They are magnificent!" agreed his wife.

"If they cannot see us," asked the sculptor, "Would they still be able to hear us? What if you called to them?"

Greesha took a deep breath and shouted loudly.

"Milites!" she called in Latin, "Potesne me audire?"

There was no reaction.

"They don't hear me," she announced.

"What if you shouted your very loudest?" asked the sculptor.

Greesha gulped in air, filling her lungs to their maximum capacity, and cupped her hands either side of her mouth. No sooner had she done so, than she dropped her hands and released her breath.

"They are gone, now, so I am unable to try, but I am quite certain that they are not meant to hear me, yet."

"Yet?"

"Yes," Greesha replied, evidently puzzled, "It would seem that way."

"Did you see," asked Marie, "When they departed, how they faded away and dissolved?"

"Yes. One moment they were there and the next they were gone. It was like a puff of steam from a kettle disappearing into the air."

"My grandmother saw them, once or twice," Marie confided, "She was very sensitive to things from the other world, and she said that it was just the way you describe."

"Was your grandmother afraid of them?"

"No."

"Are you afraid of them?"

"No."

"Neither of us are afraid of them," the sculptor explained, speaking for both of them, "But they can, at times, make us feel a little..."

"Melancholy," his wife finished for him.

"Yes, melancholy."

"Due to their distress?" Greesha enquired, "Because they are fretting and anxious?"

"Yes," they both replied at once.

"Then we must strive to release them."

"Release them? How do you mean?"

"From purgatory."

"Purgatory?"

"Yes," Greesha confirmed, "For they are in a place that is neither this world nor the next world. They are trapped in a realm that is in-between."

"How do we free them?"

"I have no idea."

"Then what can be done?"

"We must talk to the priest when he arrives."

"Which priest?" asked the sculptor, "We are not expecting any priest."

With this, he turned to his wife and she looked as mystified as he.

"We don't know who you mean."

"Think who it might be that I mean," Greesha implored, "Think back. It might be a long time ago."

"Father McCafferty!" Marie exclaimed, "The priest who blessed the well."

"I don't think the well ever *needed* blessing!" scowled her husband.

"None-the-less," she said, resting a hand affectionately on his arm, "He blessed it for us."

The sculptor gave the look of a chastised child.

There was a sound. Everybody stopped and listened. They had all heard the same thing. A little way behind them there was the noise of shifting pebbles underfoot as somebody struggled up the steep path to the top of the rise. This was followed by the sound of somebody grabbing the overhanging branches of a tree for support.

"My feet are aching," called a plaintive voice, to nobody in particular, "And my right heel is throbbing as though somebody were using it for an anvil."

All eyes turned towards the voice.

"I hope and I wish and I pray," it said, "That there is a good reason for me needing to be here."

"We have company!" said Greesha, brightly.

"Nobody comes up here but us," replied the sculptor.

The trio waited expectantly and it was not long before a head came into view, bobbing and swaying, as its owner laboured up the last dozen strides.

"Father McCafferty!" Marie exclaimed, "We were just talking about you, this very minute!"

"You were?" he panted, stopping to recover his breath, "I looked up here, from the road down below, and something told me that I should be atop this path."

"It did?" asked Greesha.

"Yes, young lassie, it did and you of all people should understand."

"Should I?"

"Yes, you should. You are well familiar with sudden impulses that drive you to do things that you cannot properly explain."

"I am?"

"Yes," replied the priest, with a warm smile, "You are."

"How could you know this?"

"So, you do not deny it?"

"No," she conceded, "But please know that it is as much an affliction as it is any kind of blessing."

"You are *speaking* to one of the afflicted," the priest laughed.

"A fellow sufferer?"

At this, he laughed even more.

"Yes, for suffer we do! Do we not?"

"How can you know this?" Greesha protested, "We have only just met. I do not so much as recall passing you in the street."

"I think, perhaps, you are receiving a little bit of your own medicine," the priest chuckled.

Greesha gave him a twinkling smile.

"My dear friends," said Father McCafferty turning to the sculptor and his wife, "Would it be rude of me to ask for a favour? Would it be possible for this young lady and I to talk in private for a few moments?"

The couple assured him that he was welcome to do so. The priest thanked them, copiously, and – placing a hand on Greesha's back – gently guided her forward to walk with him as he strolled to stand a short distance away.

"Why am I here?" he asked her in a kindly voice.

Greesha closed her eyes and connected with the person she had started to call her *other self*.

"Because you are needed," she replied.

"And why are you here?"

Greesha closed her eyes, again, for a moment.

"Because I, too, am needed."

"And why have they brought you up here, to this particular place, far from anywhere?" he asked, gesturing towards the sculptor and his wife.

This time, Greesha did not need to close her eyes, because the answer came to her in a flash.

"Because it was necessary."

"That is exactly so."

"And what is necessary," she added, "Is what must happen."

"We all have a place in the grand scheme of things and nothing that has ever happened has happened without a reason for it."

"Yes, just so," she agreed.

"Everyone must obey those things that must be, but you and I do so more willingly than most."

Greesha smiled, feeling that the holy man was some kind of kindred spirit.

"There are more things in this world," she said, "And in the world beyond this world, than we could ever begin to imagine."

"That is a very wise head you have on your very young shoulders."

"I am as I am," she declared, lowering her head to look down at herself and raising her palms in a gesture of resignation, "I am no more certain of myself than anyone who might chance to come across me."

"You were always good with words," the priest grinned.

"We have only just met," she objected, for a second time.

"Have we?" he asked, slightly amused, "You? I? Us?"

Greesha gave him an annoyed look and then, placing her hands on her hips, lifted her chin in defiance. This only served to amuse him more. Seeing her displeasure at his response, he relented.

"Little girl," he explained apologetically, "I have met another you in another time."

"In the future?" she asked, nervously.

"Far in the future."

"When?"

"The year eight thirty-five."

She gasped in surprise.

"Tell me," he urged, "You know of that year?"

"I have dreamed of it."

"If I am right – and I know that I am – you have *more* than dreamed of it."

"Yes," she nodded, "Perhaps so."

"Not just perhaps."

"No, not just perhaps," she conceded, giving him a weak smile.

"The year eight thirty-five is no longer how it once was."

Greesha gave a little moan and slapped a hand to her mouth. Her distress was evident.

"You recall it?" he asked.

"Yes," she nodded, "I remember waking up, suddenly, from a dream."

"How did you feel?"

"I was in a state of panic. I was horrified."

The priest nodded, sympathetically.

"It is all coming back to me," she revealed, "I remember asking myself out loud: *'What have I just done?'* but there was no need for that question because I knew full well what I had done. I had dreamed like that – far too many times before – not to know. It was the kind of dream where everything was so vivid and so real that it felt as if it were actually happening."

"And?" he coaxed.

"I remember telling myself that anything that happened in that kind of dream actually **had** happened. I remember groaning as I recalled what I had done in the dream. I remember cursing myself."

"What did you say?"

"I recall saying: *'God forgive me for what I have done!'*"

"What *had* you done?"

"In that dream I had gone to the year eight thirty-five. There, I saved the life of the last Pictish princess of pure blood. She should have been the last of her line, with no children, but – because of me – she married King Kenneth MacAlpin."

Father McCafferty nodded, slowly, as he processed what was the final confirmation of what he had already suspected.

"By saving her," he announced, "The king's Pictish bloodline – or rather, now, *their Pictish bloodline* – will survive and continue into the future for at least another eight centuries, rather than merging and fading away into the Gaelic bloodlines."

"You are certain?"

"Yes, I know it and you know it, too."

"I do?"

"Yes," he smiled, "For when I said that we had met in the future, I didn't say that it was only the once."

# CHAPTER 29

Balgair McRory gave his horse a second apple and then a third. When the beast nudged him to beg for more, he had to push its head away to restrain it.

"You've had enough!" he insisted, "Any more and you'll have a poorly belly."

The horse stood stock still and regarded him with the most heartbreakingly sad brown eyes.

"Very well," grumbled Balgair, relenting, "But look away from me after this one. It's the last."

The animal snorted as if it understood, took the apple from Balgair's outstretched hand and immediately turned its head away.

"I can still see your left eye," Balgair objected, "And I know that you can see me."

It was the horse, now, that grumbled – making a muffled chuntering noise – before reluctantly turning itself to stand at an angle from him.

"That's better," its rider confirmed, "But no sneaking a look. None of this food that I am packing is for you to eat any sooner than this afternoon."

The horse stamped its rear hooves and muttered to itself.

"Don't test me!" Balgair warned, "Or I'll take this whip and I'll beat you with it."

He picked up a whip and held it out into the horse's field of vision. The horse didn't flinch but, instead, made a long noise, ending with a whinny, that seemed to approximate laughter.

"Mock me at your peril!" Balgair snapped.

The horse shook its head around – left to right and up and down – before repeating the previous noise.

"Laugh all you want," Balgair glowered, "But I could easily turn nasty and violent at the drop of an acorn."

This time, they both laughed. The horse turned and buffeted him with its head and rubbed its ear against his arm. Balgair promptly stroked and tousled the horse, causing it to make a noise of pleasure and encouragement. Balgair began to scratch it behind the ear it had offered and the horse rolled its eyes, comically, causing him to burst out laughing. After a minute or so, Balgair stopped scratching and turned to resume the job of filling canvas bags with provisions. The horse promptly made a noise of complaint. Balgair resumed the scratching. After a while he stopped, again, but quickly addressed the horse before it could object.

"I have things to do and I can't stand scratching you all day. If you still want scratching, go and find a tree and rub up against it."

The horse sighed and chuntered a little, before lowering its head and beginning to crop the grass.

Somebody nearby deliberately scuffed the ground with their boots to announce their approach. As Balgair turned around, he heard The MacDonald call out to him.

"Horses are sometimes more like people than people!" he exclaimed jovially.

It was clear to Balgair that he had heard at least part of his 'conversation' with his steed.

"Yes," Balgair agreed, "And they often make a lot more sense than people."

The two men exchanged amiable but entirely worthless conversation for a minute or so before the Clan Chief decided to declare the true reason for his presence.

"Our scouts have picked up signs of large numbers of Campbells setting out towards the north east. A few of the trails are weakly disguised with the intention of them being discovered. These lead nowhere, having been created solely for the purpose of confusing us and wasting our time."

"Should I get ahead of them and ambush them?"

The MacDonald grinned at his enthusiasm, but waved a hand to restrain him.

"No, let them be. We know their mission and we will, in the end, defeat them. I have plenty of troops out there, already, to harass and delay them and to thin out their ranks. They'll not reach their destination without losing at least one in five of their men."

"What if I am attacked by them, along the way?"

"Defend yourself. Kill them. Survive. Move on as soon as you can. Don't tarry to chase down any Campbells who flee."

"I will do exactly as you say."

"When you reach Boat of Garten, that is where the real battle will occur. Kill every Campbell you possibly can, before the Queen of the West stops you. I want the battlefield piled high with their bodies and the fields and glens around it strewn with the corpses of those who turned and ran."

"It will be so."

"If she gives you orders that conflict with mine, hers are the orders you must obey."

"I will."

"You must obey her every command without hesitation. Her word is the law to you and your men. Her word is your religion."

"I will remember."

The Chief of the Clan MacDonald hesitated, opening his mouth a couple of times to speak, but failing to find the right words. Eventually, with a note of exasperation, he seemed to settle for expressing himself without any care for caution.

"She is dangerous. She is a killer."

Balgair blinked in surprise.

"Do *not* underestimate her," The MacDonald warned, "For her skill with a sword, a dagger or any blade is shocking."

Balgair attempted a reply, but he was cut short.

"She is fast. She is very fast. She is faster than anyone you will have ever faced."

"Faster than Wallace or Gillyn?" Balgair asked, incredulously.

The MacDonald let out a scornful snort.

"She would make both of them look tired and feeble."

Balgair raised his eyebrows as a spark of realisation passed across his face.

"Yet, you are sending troops to protect her?"

The MacDonald looked weary at his question.

"The Campbells will send hundreds of men against her. I want you to put as many of them into the ground as you can. If only a dozen of them make it through then – with her by your side – the two of you will still stand a chance.”

“The two of us? Will she not take refuge?”

“Take refuge?” The MacDonald laughed, “Absolutely not! While you must protect her at all costs she, too, will protect you. That is her way. She is a true Warrior Queen from a line of Warrior Queens.”

“I understand,” replied Balgair, still looking a little dubious.

“I don’t think you do.”

Balgair bit his tongue.

“Unfortunately,” The MacDonald bemoaned, “You will not appreciate her until you encounter her.”

“She sounds fiercesome.”

The MacDonald gave him a sharp look, uncertain – for a moment – of his sincerity.

“Fiercesome describes her exactly. Your challenge will be how to protect her. She will not shrink from danger, no matter what the odds.”

Balgair looked puzzled.

“She is a young girl of nineteen. Will she not fear for her life?” he asked.

The MacDonald laughed derisively.

“She’ll fear nothing and – believe me – her age has nothing what-so-ever to do with it.”

Balgair’s face betrayed his puzzlement.

“Heed me, Balgair, when I say this: She fears only God and the Devil and, even then, I think she has precious little respect for the Devil.”

The two men laughed heartily.

“I will protect her life with the last drop of my blood,” Balgair vowed.

“Aye. Good lad. Do that,” he replied, obviously distracted.

“What is it, My Chief?”

“Serving her will be the greatest honour of your life.”

“You hold her in great esteem.”

“Aye, I do, and so will you. I guarantee it.”

"If you say I will, then I will, for sure."

"Have a safe journey, Balgair McRory, and look after your men."

"Thank you. I will."

The two men shook hands and The MacDonald turned to depart, but suddenly gave a little laugh and turned back.

"If she ever offers to wrestle with you," he quipped, "You had best decline, for the sake of your own dignity!"

Balgair looked confused.

"She is a big woman?" he asked, gesturing with his arms bowed out either side of his hips to indicate a prodigious breadth.

"She is indeed. She is huge. A giant, in fact."

Balgair failed to control his face in time to hide his disappointment. The MacDonald, on seeing it, made a deep rumbling noise in his throat and chest as an audible reprimand. Then, he stepped forward and pushed Balgair hard in the chest, causing him to stagger backwards.

"She is a giant not in her physical stature, but in her status and prestige," he scolded, "If we're discussing her size, my head and my two arms weigh more than she does."

Balgair's attempt to hide his joy at this information was entirely unsuccessful.

"You," the Clan Chief admonished, "Would do better to respect a woman for her worth rather than for how nice she is to look at."

Balgair stuck out his bottom lip and hung his head, pretending to be offended. This drew another rumbling sound for his trouble. His jest had clearly not amused.

The leader of the Clan MacDonald strode two paces away before stopping, again, and turning to add: "She is *very nice* to look at, by the way."

Balgair beamed at him. His leader, disregarding the distance between them, raised an arm and drew back his hand as if preparing to slap him across the side of the head. Balgair made an exaggerated pretence of cowering. This time, The MacDonald relented in his ill humour and laughed. Balgair laughed too, but mostly from relief.

# CHAPTER 30

As he walked to gather his men, Balgair McRory cursed himself and made a mental note to take a firm grip of his tongue the next time he might speak to The MacDonald. He resolved to permanently apply his better nature to his behaviour, in order to avoid conveying any further wrong impressions of his attitude to women.

Then, he froze.

He was being sent to protect the Queen of the West. A woman. A woman who commanded the loyalty, the respect and the absolute reverence of his Clan Chief. Balgair immediately spun around and hurried after The MacDonald. When he caught up with him, with just a couple of paces separating them, the Laird MacDonald stopped and, without turning, grasped the hilt of his sword. Balgair veered off the path to circle around him, leaving a wide berth, and approached him from the front.

"My Chief," he said, his eyes downcast, "I would never show contempt for a woman based upon her size, for my own mother was no wee, skinny waif, herself."

The MacDonald said nothing and only listened.

"I regret how I must have sounded and I apologise."

The MacDonald nodded, slowly, appearing to accept his apology begrudgingly.

"I swear it is the truth. I swear it upon this steel," declared Balgair, drawing his sword, dropping to his knees and kissing the crosspiece of his weapon.

The MacDonald briskly and firmly raised his arm and waved his hand to left and right as if slicing the air. Balgair looked up at the hand, confusion written across his face.

"Hear me lad: By now, there will be at least two or three archers – and maybe as many as half a dozen – with their bows drawn tight and an arrow aimed directly at you. If you wish to reach a ripe old age, I suggest that you make this the last time that you bare a blade in my presence like that."

Looking nervous, Balgair very, very slowly returned his blade to its sheath.

"Tell me, Balgair, do you know why you're not already laying dead in the dirt?"

Balgair pursed his lips and frowned, making no response.

"Because, lad, I am a good judge of men and those archers know it. Therefore, they decided that you deserved at least a few more seconds of life – in order for them to gauge your true intentions – before they filled you so full of arrows that you would look like a hedgehog with its quills attached by a drunkard."

Balgair looked chastened.

"Too many young men, of your sort of age, like to use jokes and sly remarks to make pretence that they are rough and unpolished in their ways. This, they believe, makes them more manly. As often as not this will involve showing a calculated disdain for women."

Balgair opened his mouth to protest but The Chief of the Clan raised a hand to silence him.

"This is not you. This is not your way. This is, however, the effect of your being exposed to such behaviour, witnessing it and not resisting it. Be a model for your men. They were carefully selected, as were you. Show them by your actions what you believe and they will adopt your values as their own."

Balgair nodded.

"Your worrying what impression you had left on me is a good thing. Now, go and make an impression on your men."

Balgair made to stand, but – before he could – the Chieftain roared with laughter and he dropped back to his knees.

"So full of arrows," he repeated, "That you would look like a hedgehog with its quills attached by a drunkard."

Balgair held his breath.

"That was a good use of words," The MacDonald congratulated himself, "I must use that phrase, sometime, at a banquet or something."

With this, he straightened his tunic and cleared his throat.

Understanding that he had just been dismissed, Balgair McRory rose to his feet, saluted, and made off to muster his cavalry.

# CHAPTER 31

"My dreams of the future sometimes worry me," Greesha confessed.

"I know what you mean," Father McCafferty replied.

"You said that you had met me more than once in the future?"

"Yes. I have," he enthused, "For this thing that you do, you are going to become very, very good at it!"

"I am?"

"I, for myself, am merely splashing around in the shallows. I am still within an arm's length of the shore. You, on the other hand, young lady, are way out into the deep water."

She shook her head, uncertainly.

"Father, I don't yet really understand exactly what it is that happens to me or what are the rules and boundaries."

"I have moved myself between places and between times, but it has only ever been as an observer. I cannot project my entire self."

"I was unable to do so for a while, but it somehow came to me."

"How long did it take you?"

Greesha blushed and looked flustered.

"It took me only a day or two."

The priest applauded her and wrapped her in a hug.

"You have a gift!" he declared, "A wonderful gift!"

"It is *we* who have a gift," she corrected, "And, in having it, we also have a curse."

His answer was a scowl. It was not a topic the priest relished discussing. Releasing her, he nodded towards the sculptor and his wife.

"They will be wondering what it is that we are discussing."

"Perhaps I should tell them that you are my long-lost uncle?"

"I think they know enough about the both of us, already, for them to be hard to convince."

There was a long pause, during which they both pondered the same question. It was a question that neither had got around to asking. As if reading his mind, Greesha asked it.

"What about the army from the past who march up and down the field and across the glen?"

"Yes, what about them, indeed."

"The things that happen to us, they are always for a purpose?"

"Aye, girlie, I believe they are."

"Then for what purpose are we – the two of us – here?"

Father McCafferty looked thoughtful for a moment.

"To give them peace," he said, "To put them to rest from their torment."

"How shall we do that? They cannot hear me. How can they be helped if I cannot even talk to them?"

"I do not know," he shrugged.

"Are we not told that the force sent into this world, to do the will of the mighty force beyond and before this world, is more powerful than anything we can ever imagine?"

"Aye, we are."

"Then such a force must be able to let us know or show us the means by which we can do the things it wishes."

"That would be sensible to suppose."

"Maybe our hosts know?"

"I doubt it."

"Maybe, Father, our hosts don't know that they know?"

"How would that be?"

"Everything happens for a reason. Maybe there is something that has already happened but has yet to show itself as being the reason?"

"Lead on," said the priest, motioning with a swirl of his arm towards the sculptor and his wife.

They walked back to rejoin the couple, where they were greeted by expectant looks.

"Have you reached a conclusion?" asked the sculptor.

Greesha replied to the question with another question.

"Is there anywhere in your house, or around and about it, that feels different? A place that has a particular aura?"

She was promptly greeted by expressions of disbelief.

"How could you know that?" asked the sculptor, "Did you sense it yourself?"

"No. Perhaps I was too occupied by other things."

"It is the fireplace in the main living area," his wife revealed, "We are both – my husband and I – drawn to the great oak beam that is set into the stonework above it. There is something about it that neither of us has ever been able to explain."

"Can we see it?"

"Yes, of course, let's go back to the house."

With this, the little party of four followed the trail back down to the grand house, filed through its doorway and assembled in the main chamber in front of the fire.

"I understand what you mean," Greesha declared, leaning across the hearth and placing a hand on the stout wooden beam that spanned the fireplace.

Spontaneously, the sculptor and his wife came to stand either side of her and began to stroke the wooden beam. Unwilling to be excluded, Father McCafferty joined them.

"There is something about this beam," he said, resting a palm against it, "It is almost as if…."

The others all turned to look at him as he searched for the words he wanted.

"Almost as if it were drawing us to it," he finished.

"Yes," they all agreed, each in turn.

"How old is this house?" asked Greesha.

"Over a hundred and fifty years, I think," the sculptor contemplated, "Perhaps even two hundred. My family built it."

"The fireplace, however," his wife added, "Came from an older house, built up beyond the ridge, on the slope of the glen."

"This beam, too, is from the old house?" asked Greesha, eagerly.

"Yes, the beam was brought here along with the rest of the fireplace. People who know the local history say that the old house stood there for almost five centuries."

Father McCafferty and Greesha locked eyes and gasped.

"It has something inside it!" they both said at exactly the same moment.

"What is it?" asked Marie.

The priest and the little girl exchanged a glance, then both shrugged.

"Whatever it is, how do we get it out?" Marie enquired.

The previous shrug was repeated.

"With levers, poles and rods, amongst other things, I should think," offered the sculptor, "I have those kind of tools."

"Not a saw or an axe?" Father McCafferty asked.

"No. We don't cut into the beam from the front. We first remove the stone blocks set into the fireplace at either end of it, then we can drill into the beam from the sides."

With this decided, they went about putting the plan into action, laying down sheets to protect the carpet from the dust and debris before assembling the required tools on a bench.

With great care they began to chisel away and remove the mortar surrounding the stone block to the left of the fireplace. Levering rods were then inserted into the newly formed gaps to take the weight, while ropes and wooden rollers were pushed between them. Gradually, the mortar was dug out deeper and deeper into the gaps until it was all gone. The sculptor then drove additional levering rods along the back of the stone to create a channel, and then used a stout iron bar, to dislodge it. The rollers began to turn and the solid block of stone was eased forward.

"Now," the sculptor explained, "We place sacks of sand, one on top of the other, to build a tower in front of the stone. The tower will be only a little lower than the stone and will be used to support it."

"I have a question," said Father McCafferty, holding up his hand as if he were a student in a schoolroom, "How do we get the stone onto the tower of sacks?"

"I will show you," the sculptor winked, "When we have made the tower."

The sculptor and his makeshift team of engineers quickly constructed the tower of sacks, each filled with coarse sand, until the required height was reached.

"Now we take a sack filled with very fine sand," said the sculptor, "And we wedge it between the stone and the top of the tower."

The said sack was dragged in front of the tower and lifted into position to test its size. It was slightly too small. The sack was placed back on the ground, its neck untied, and several more scoops sand added to it. It was still too small. The process was repeated until if fitted perfectly.

"Now, finally, we get to move the stone," the sculptor told them, "Using this."

He produced a wooden tube with a narrow hole down the middle of it, into which was inserted a metal spike.

Father McCafferty looked at him, dubiously, and knotted his brows.

"All will be revealed," the sculptor insisted.

Under his direction, the stone was levered forward and out, until its weight rested against the sack of fine sand. The sculptor, then, fetched a mallet and, holding the wooden tube against the fabric of the sack, tapped the tube with the mallet to drive it through. Once in place, he removed the metal spike and the sand began to run out through the tube, quickly forming a pile on the floor. As the sand emptied from the sack, the stone began to slowly descend until, with the sack completely empty, it rested atop the tower.

The priest and Greesha broke into applause. Marie applauded, too, but mostly out of politeness, for she had seen this feat performed many times before.

"Wonderful!" exclaimed the priest.

"Splendid!" agreed Greesha.

The sculptor made a lavish, theatrical bow whilst extravagantly flourishing an imaginary hat. This was greeted by further applause, by joyful laughter and by deliberately excessive pats on the back.

Once the outburst of camaraderie had subsided, the sculptor cleared away a layer of dust and rock fragments to address the end of the prodigious beam. There, he quickly made a discovery.

# CHAPTER 32

The sculptor peered intently at the end of the beam.

"This beam has had a hole cut into its end," he pointed out, "And a round lid inserted, like a plug in a barrel."

They all pressed close to see the thing he described and the priest, raising a hand, knocked on the lid as if it were somebody's front door.

"I don't think anybody is at home," quipped Marie, cupping a hand to her ear.

"If not *somebody* at home," her husband responded with a smile, "Then surely *something* is at home."

"And waiting for us to call," Greesha added.

Without delay, a knife was inserted into the tiny gap between the lid and the beam and worked back and forth until the lid began to loosen. As soon as the aperture was wide enough, the very tip of an axe blade was inserted and the lid pried out of its centuries old resting place.

"We need a lantern!" exclaimed the priest, excitedly.

The sculptor turned to his wife to fetch one and she, in return, gave him a withering look of disdain. She did not speak, but the words: *"Am I your servant?"* were very clearly communicated.

Giving a little laugh, the sculptor gently gripped his wife's head by placing one of his huge hands either side of it and planted a kiss firmly on her lips.

"If you look in the ice shed, we have a spare lantern there," she told him, "On a hook by the corner shelf."

The sculptor disappeared outside for a minute or so and returned with the lantern. Holding it up with one hand, he lifted its glass sleeve with the other, to expose the wick. His wife obliged him by lighting a wooden splint from the log fire and touching the flame to the wick.

Handing the lantern to Father McCafferty to hold, the sculptor reached his arm inside the beam.

"There's definitely something in here," he announced, beginning to withdraw a long roll of sail cloth.

The cloth had been liberally daubed with some kind of substance that may, long ago, have been thick and waxy, but which had been rendered hard and brittle by the effects of time.

Placing the bundle on the floor he began to remove its outer coating. It was like peeling the shell from a hard boiled egg. Next, he untied the cord that held the bundle closed and pulled off the thick fabric. Beneath it, there was a preservative jacket of goo that had remained surprisingly runny. Once the goo had been removed, a pale-yellow substance was revealed. The look and feel of it resembled something like a block of soap.

It took them almost an hour of painstaking and diligent care to strip back all of the protective layers before they were able to reveal the object inside.

"Somebody put this here quite deliberately," the sculptor marvelled, "Intending that, one day, it would be found undamaged."

"They invested an enormous amount of effort into preserving this thing," Marie pointed out, "So it was clearly important to them that it did not decay and that it remained in working order."

"You are absolutely right," agreed the priest, "There is no other explanation."

Greesha knelt and rested both her palms against the object. Closing her eyes, she concentrated hard.

"It is *very* old," she said.

"How old?"

"It is ancient."

"How old is that?"

"It dates back to the earliest times of the Romans."

# CHAPTER 33

"It belonged to a Roman Legion." said Greesha, still resting her hands against the find, "It was hidden to prevent its capture by the enemy during a challenging campaign of conquest."

She remained silent, her face contorted with effort, as she absorbed further inspiration. After she had not spoken for some time, the sculptor was unable to contain his curiosity.

"What more can you tell us?" he asked.

Greesha jolted, as if he had just slapped her, and her eyes sprang open.

"It is a tragedy," she announced, "A terrible error that cost the lives of many soldiers."

Much to the disappointment of her audience, she fell silent, again. They waited anxiously for more to be revealed and they were pleased when her attention returned a lot sooner than it had before.

"The Legion who owned this artefact advanced a little too far. They did not show sufficient caution. They left themselves at risk. As a result, they were cut off from their other forces and became surrounded."

Her audience were agog at her words.

"A desperate battle was fought. It lasted many hours. At the end of it, because of their dogged determination, their ferocious spirit and their iron clad discipline, the Roman army was able to endure. They succeeded in turning what was a looming defeat into a narrow but very costly victory. Their enemies retreated, but they did not pursue them, for the Romans had nobody left fit to do anything but collapse on the ground in exhaustion."

Greesha looked from face to face, noting her listeners' expressions of dread.

"The support they had summoned never arrived. The wrong map had been given to them. Somebody had accidentally despatched them with a map that referred to somewhere half a day's ride away. One hundred and five Roman soldiers survived from the one thousand that had marched to battle and none of them were able to blow the horn to signal victory."

"So, the dead that we have witnessed marching," Father McCafferty said, "Never knew that the battle had been won."

"But they will forever blame themselves for the dreadful loss of life," the sculptor added, "And forever strive to find a way to reach their comrades."

"And, in this case," his wife pointed out, "We really do mean forever."

"So," said Father McCafferty, "Somebody very purposely hid this beautiful thing away, entombing it in a slab of oak."

Greesha closed her eyes tightly shut and clenched her teeth and her hands with the exertion of concentration.

"They believed that one day somebody would discover it," she announced.

"How could they be sure?" Marie enquired, "It was very well concealed and, to my certain knowledge, no word was left about it for future generations."

"They left it for us," Greesha replied.

"For us?"

"Yes, for us. For the very people who are gathered here, today."

"How is that possible?"

"They had faith that the right people would find it, one day."

"How could they have known?"

"They had a Seer," said Greesha, brightly, with a sudden smile.

"They must have been a very gifted Seer."

"Not as gifted as I would have liked them to have been."

"You know them?"

"Yes. I know them. I have only just realised that I know them."

Everybody looked at her, hardly daring to breathe.

"It was me," said Greesha.

"It was *you*?" asked Marie, incredulously.

"I dreamed of them, but – apparently – it wasn't a dream! It was real. Or real enough. Or sufficiently like real to, somehow, become real."

The priest chortled, evidently amused by her attempts to make sense of her situation.

"I have been in the same predicament many times," he told her, "Not quite sure what was a dream and what was so far beyond a dream that it pierced another realm."

The sculptor and his wife both looked aghast.

"You understand what she means?" the sculptor asked Father McCafferty, using the same tone of voice that a person might employ if someone had just claimed to be a tree, "You have done those kinds of things yourself?"

"Yes," the priest confirmed.

"You are a man of God," Marie protested, "And you dabble in magic?"

"Magic?" Father McCafferty exclaimed, "No, not magic!"

"What then?"

"Merely things that belong to another kind of existence. One that is both of this world and beyond this world. A power that shuns the boundaries that constrain our mortal flesh."

Marie frowned, as if not entirely convinced.

"My wife's family," her husband offered, "Are strict about beliefs relating to…"

"The Realms of Darkness!" she interjected.

Greesha laughed and Marie looked offended.

"There is no darkness here," Greesha insisted, "Nor could there ever be!"

Marie knotted her brows and looked baffled.

"There are churches, abbeys and monasteries that have less divine spirit about them than here where you live, and it swirls all around this place, invisibly, in waves and in billowing clouds."

"It does?"

"Yes! This is a refuge. This is a bastion. This is a fortress. Only good can exist, here."

Marie looked pleased.

"This fireplace," Greesha announced, gesturing with a sweep of her arm, "Is built to hide the original purpose of its stones."

"And what was that?"

"These stones once formed an altar in a holy place."

Marie's expression was transformed into one of delight.

"This came from a holy place?" she enquired.

"From one holy place to another holy place."

"Truly?"

"Yes, in a different time and in a different situation," Greesha advised, closing her eyes and concentrating, "This was a place of safety for good people fleeing harm. People escaping persecution. This was established by monks as a sanctuary."

"I can feel it," said Father McCafferty.

Everybody nodded, sensing the same thing.

"It now makes perfect sense," the sculptor suggested, "That the Roman soldiers should have been drawn to bring the thing they regarded as so precious to such a place as they did to hide it."

The attention of all returned to the gleaming bronze object they had uncovered.

A sudden inspiration seizing him, Father McCafferty clapped his hands in delight.

"Those Roman soldiers may not be able to hear your shouts or calls," he told Greesha, enthusiastically, "But there is a very good chance that this device might make itself heard by them!"

"What is this thing called?" asked Marie, stroking the shining metal.

"They would have called it a tuba," replied Father McCafferty, "But we, today, would call it a horn."

"It is a very grand horn."

"A horn with a forlorn and truly haunting sound."

"You have heard one?"

"I have," replied the priest, looking slightly pleased with himself, "As I like to regard myself as something of an authority on the history of this region."

"Could you play this horn, Father?"

"I believe I could."

At this, Greesha put up a hand, bringing a halt to the conversation.

"I feel that there is even more to our being here than just this," she said.

"More?" Father McCafferty asked, looking quizzical.

A moment later, her meaning dawned on him. He nodded his head and, lifting his rough-spun cassock around his knees, he deposited himself, cross legged, on the ground. Greesha sat down opposite him in the same position. Without bothering to offer any explanation, the two lowered their heads and started to concentrate their minds. Jointly, they began searching for inspiration on a higher plane.

The sculptor and his wife shrugged and went to sit on a nearby bench. They were both resigned to biding their time as they waited for the attention of their guests to return. After several minutes there was a loud noise as Father McCafferty slapped his thigh.

"I have it!" he cried.

"You truly do," Greesha agreed.

"What do you have?" called the sculptor.

"I have the reason why these men who wander the field, up yonder, must be released from their torment."

"Which is?" Marie urged.

"Which is that, just as I am tied to be a priest again in a future life, a vital number of these Roman soldiers are tied, one day, to be soldiers again."

The sculptor stood up and, groaning, threw up his hands in dismay.

"It would help us, Father, if you could strive to make your words a little less mysterious and a little more understandable."

"Of course," the priest promised, taking no offence, "I will do my very best."

Rubbing his hands together, as if this would conjure plain speaking, the priest began to relate what he and Greesha had just, together, managed to learn.

"The souls of people who live their lives full of virtue and goodness, can hope to see Paradise at the end of their life. The souls of people who live their lives full of evil and wickedness, can hope for nothing other than eternal damnation."

There was general nodding at this.

"The souls of those people who live their lives just short of virtue and goodness, but far distant from evil and wickedness, can – it is said – be born again, into another life, so that they may endeavour to do better."

More nodding.

"The souls of some of these Roman soldiers are worthy of another life and another chance at reaching Heaven. They will make good of that opportunity, when it presents itself, and they will obtain eternal bliss. It is already written in their fates. In doing so, they will change the future of these lands."

"So we *must* release them," the sculptor declared.

"Or we will change the future of those who come after us," Greesha agreed.

Father McCafferty patted the horn, affectionately.

"We need to build a small fire in the yard," he announced, "So that we can melt and pour away whatever other substances were put inside this thing to preserve it."

"I will gather the kindling," Greesha announced, "And I will gather some smaller logs and sticks to build the fire."

"I will assist her," Marie offered.

"And we," said her husband, waving to the priest to include him, "Will get this instrument ready to melt the remaining wax out of it."

With a shared enthusiasm, they set about their work.

After ten minutes, Greesha stopped and offered her apologies.

"Please excuse me," she implored, "For I have a pressing matter that is about to arise. One that needs my urgent attention."

The little group watched as she walked to the wood shed and stopped with a hand resting on the latch.

"I think I will be able to concentrate better in darkness," she declared, stepping inside and closing the door behind her.

# CHAPTER 34

After insisting that his men check absolutely everything for both a second and a third time, Balgair McRory reluctantly gave them the order to set off.

Their gleaming ceremonial armour had been stashed in canvas bags, carefully padded with straw and wood shavings, then loaded into carts. It had been a challenge of wills for him to get them all to take off the armour, so enthralled had they been with it. Over and over they had begged Balgair for just one last moment to strut and preen and admire themselves. It had been more like organising children, he reflected, than soldiers.

Ahead of them, the sun was urging them on, sailing across an almost cloudless blue sky. The birds sang at the tops of their voices from every hedge and bush to serenade them. The trees swayed, swooshing and whooshing, whenever they passed beneath them. The grass undulated like a green sea, either side of the track, as the wind chased across the meadows.

Balgair had, earlier, shaken hands with, hugged and slapped the back of the man who rode to his left. He, now, subdued the urge to jump from his horse and do the same, again. The man, Sachairi, had been his childhood best friend and had just been recalled from Northumberland by The MacDonald, in order to join Balgair as his Second-in-Command.

"You and I will go ahead," Balgair announced, "And we will catch up with the rearmost of our scouts."

"As you command," Sachairi replied, touching his brow in salute.

Balgair signalled his intentions to the men behind them. Then, spurring their horses, the two of them galloped to the bend in the road in the far distance and disappeared around it.

"This is a perfect day," Balgair declared.

"It is a glorious day."

"It is almost as if…" he began, leaving his words to hang.

"As if the gods are with us," the other finished.

"Exactly so. Be there just the one God – or even any number of them – the weather seems to be telling us that we have full approval, from on high, for our mission."

Sachairi nodded enthusiastically.

"I truly believe," he grinned, "That I was born for this day!"

"We were *all* born for this day."

The two men rode on in companionable good humour, both in high spirits and a buoyant mood. They had grown up in the same village, climbing trees together, swimming in the brook together, learning to ride horses together and running up, down and around the surrounding hills together. They had joined The MacDonald army together. They had fought their first battle together. They had been appointed to the cavalry together.

Neither could think of a single thing that could quell their joy on this glorious day… until it happened.

Sachairi's elation was pricked like a bubble as he suddenly stiffened and caught his breath.

"What is it?" asked his friend.

Sachairi did not reply, but only stared ahead of them at the gap in the trees. Balgair followed the direction of his gaze and uttered a curse. There, at the edge of the road, stood Sachairi's bullying and tyrannical uncle.

Sachairi's mouth and throat became dry and he found that he couldn't swallow. He could feel his pulse beating fast in his neck and temples. His heart pounded in his chest like a boulder were being bounced off it.

The man who stood ahead of them, by the road, had viciously beaten Sachairi as a child and had made his life an utter misery. He had broken Sachairi's spirit, crushed his belief in himself and – by his shouting and bellowing – had reduced him to tears. This had been from the earliest age he could remember. Sachairi's life had been made a nightmare and he had been compelled to make up constant excuses for the bruises his uncle inflicted on him. He had claimed to have had so many falls and mishaps that his parents had become suspicious. Sachairi had finally pretended to be the victim of a group of bullies from nearby villages and insisted that they regularly laid in wait for him and set about him at every opportunity. Balgair, much against his wishes and despite his protests, had eventually been persuaded to support this tale and invent instances that he had witnessed.

Eventually, Sachairi had been sent to Dunfermline to study. His time away had been completely blissful, but – when he returned – his uncle had redoubled his beatings. A year or so later, he was despatched to Inverness to study. The whole time he was there he had nightmares, crying out in his sleep and waking up bathed in sweat. Eventually, the time came for him to set off back home. He had become so sick with worry during the journey that he was diverted to the infirmary at a local monastery along their route. The monks could find nothing physically wrong with him and, after administering a series of tonics, had sent him on his way.

Balgair had met him on the North Road and pleaded with him to simply run away, but he had refused. He had begged Sachairi to release him from his oath and allow him to tell his father what was happening, but he had refused. Whatever route or avenue Balgair presented to end his friend's suffering, he would not entertain it.

In their youth, Balgair had encouraged Sachairi to join him and others who were learning to wrestle and to fight with their fists but, no matter how well he did and no matter how accomplished he became, Sachairi never had the spirit to take on his uncle.

Balgair bristled to see that very man now ahead of them on the road. He seethed with hatred and his sword hand itched to take hold of his weapon and extract revenge. Balgair knew that Sachairi was capable of defeating his uncle in any kind of struggle or combat, if only he were able to overcome his fear.

"You need to lay this ghost to rest!" snarled Balgair, leaning close to his friend.

Sachairi turned to him and looked distraught.

"I cannot," he replied.

"You must!" Balgair urged.

Suddenly their horses stopped, unbidden, and refused to move. Everything became quiet. The birds stopped singing. The trees stopped rustling. Even the swaying grass became silent. The feeling was eerie.

Out of nowhere a little girl appeared in the middle of the track.

Balgair and Sachairi blinked in disbelief and exchanged glances, seeking each other's assurance that she wasn't some kind of trick of the mind.

The little girl held up her hand and approached the side of Sachairi's horse. She spoke quietly, but firmly to him, looking directly into his eyes.

"You are no longer afraid of your uncle," she instructed.

The change in Sachairi's demeanour was instantaneous. He sat tall in his saddle, put back his shoulders and stuck out his chin.

"That man, there, needs a good thrashing," he told Balgair, dismounting from his horse, "And I intend to deliver it to him."

Balgair watched in utter astonishment as his friend strode towards his uncle. He moved with confidence and with no hesitation. There was not so much as a flicker of worry about him. His uncle, who had been standing menacingly, abruptly lost his nerve and shrank back.

Without breaking his stride and without slowing, Sachairi struck his uncle squarely on the jaw. The blow took him clean off his feet and landed him on his back. His uncle sprang back up and promptly threw a punch at his nephew. With leisurely disdain, Sachairi stepped aside, leaving his attacker's fist to connect with empty air. His uncle threw another blow. Sachairi dodged effortlessly out of reach. Another blow came and Sachairi turned his head, leaning away to evade it.

As if abruptly losing patience with the situation, Sachairi lunged at his uncle and hit him on the side of the head. The blow connected with a sickening thud, causing his uncle to collapse as if his legs had gone missing. Bending and picking him off the dirt, Sachairi flung him against a tree. Immediately retrieving him, he hauled his uncle to his feet and, holding him up by the scruff of the neck, smacked his forearm across his face, breaking his nose.

Balgair looked at the little girl. She was strangely familiar. He tilted his head to one side, then to the other, looking her up and down. She gave him a charming smile. He continued to look at her, furrowing his brow and scowling. Her grin told him that she was amused by his confusion.

Lifting her hand to intercept his gaze, she flicked her fingers open, three times, like a bursting star and made a little noise: "Ziff! Ziff! Ziff!"

She turned back to look at the combatants and Balgair followed the direction of her eyes.

To his surprise, there came a loud noise, 'Ziff!', then almost straight away, 'Ziff!', then for a third time, 'Ziff!'.

Sachairi's uncle had pulled out a vicious, curved knife and, upon raising it above his head to strike, had staggered backwards and fallen to his knees as three arrows, one after the other, struck him in the chest.

Across the dirt track, a little way up it, stood the three advanced scouts that Balgair had sent ahead of them, their empty bows still held in firing position.

Balgair turned back to the little girl but, the very moment his eyes lighted upon her, she vanished. He looked at the space where she had been standing and gawped.

# CHAPTER 35

Greesha emerged from the woodshed looking quietly pleased.

"You have attended to your matter?" asked Father McCafferty.

"I have," she replied.

"Satisfactorily?"

"Yes," she grinned, "There was a rat that needed to be killed."

The priest looked puzzled.

"And it was a rat that required your attention in particular?"

"Yes. For it was a vile rat. A rat that was tall enough to rest its chin on the top of your head."

"Oh! I see. That kind of rat!"

They both chuckled.

As if she had never been away, Greesha rejoined them in their labours. Together, they slipped the gleaming horn into a makeshift wire harness that held it at the precise distance required above the fire. Soon, a steady stream of waxy, yellow syrup began to pour out of it. When the fluid began to diminish, they moved the horn this way and that, tilting and tipping it, until nothing more came out.

"I think it is as close to being in good working order as we will ever be able to achieve," said the sculptor.

Everybody agreed.

"If our instincts are right," said Marie, "And this is what is needed, then everything we have done will have been worthwhile."

There were nods all round.

"We are here, not by chance," Greesha assured everyone, "But for this very purpose."

"We are indeed," the priest enthused, "I have no doubt about it."

Feeling full of hope, they gathered up all of the tools and equipment they had used and put them back where they belonged. Shelves, boxes and cupboards that had been rendered bare were, once more, filled with the items that had been pressed into service.

It was agreed, unanimously, that the huge gap that remained above the fireplace could wait until the following morning. Nobody had the enthusiasm to tackle it any sooner.

After a hurried meal – nobody having realised, until then, how long it had been since any of them had last eaten – they all retired to bed, completely exhausted.

Fatigue, however, was unable to suppress their excitement and they all found difficulty in getting to sleep. Arranging to rise before dawn, none of them found more than intermittent rest. To the surprise of their hosts, when Father McCafferty and Greesha were woken, they had both already washed and dressed and were fully clothed beneath their blankets.

Breakfast was rushed, an air of excitement being almost tangible throughout the meal. Despite having plenty to say, nobody spoke, fearing that they might delay setting off.

Before too long, they were carrying the ancient horn across the meadow to the base of the hills, careful to mind their footing in the dim light.

"The battle was fought beyond those mountains," Father McCafferty announced, holding up his lantern to illuminate his own face, "It took place on the flat plain that lays to the north. If we make it up to the second rise of the nearest mountain, the horn will be in a good location for it to be heard and its sound will be coming from the appropriate direction."

Everybody agreed on the wisdom of this idea.

An hour later, with the sun on the very brink of rising, they made it to their chosen location and laid the horn carefully in a position where it could be played.

"Tell me, Father McCafferty," the sculptor asked, "How did you learn to blow such an instrument as this?"

The priest looked slightly amused.

"I have never blown one in my life, but I have a feeling that this will not prove to be an obstacle."

This was met with general dismay.

"What are the notes you will blow?" asked the sculptor, "What kind of sound? Will it be some kind of a signal?"

"I have no idea."

"None at all?"

"None, but – strangely enough – I have the confidence of a man who has tripped while stood on the bank of a river and who, as he falls, is certain that he is about to hit the water."

The sculptor looked puzzled. His wife, Marie, looked unsure. Greesha looked dubious.

After a few moments, as if impervious to their scepticism, Father McCafferty clapped his hands.

"Is this the time that they are likely to appear?" he asked.

"Yes," replied the sculptor, "I hope we are fortunate."

"And that we have not climbed up here, all this way, for nothing?"

"They will appear."

"How do you know."

"I just know."

"That is good enough for me, for I *just know* that I will be able to play this thing!"

The priest took hold of the horn and placed the mouthpiece to his lips. As if waiting for their cue, the sound of marching feet began, far below them.

Father McCafferty took in a deep breath, closed his eyes and blew. The sound was like that of a lost soul. It was a heartbreakingly dismal moan. The marching stopped. Father McCafferty paused for only a second or two before he played again. This time it was with gusto, revelling in each note.

They waited, holding their breath.

They listened, straining their ears.

They prayed, silently.

Suddenly, there was a roar from the Roman army. There was cheering. There was clapping. There was stamping of feet. There was banging of shields.

"Victoriam!" shouted some of the soldiers.

They were jubilant. They were overjoyed. They were exuberant.

"What are they saying?" asked the sculptor and his wife, both speaking at the same moment.

"Victory!" replied Father McCafferty and Greesha, also both speaking at the same moment.

"They clearly understood you," the sculptor rejoiced, "You really did know what notes to blow."

The priest laughed and shook his head.

"To be perfectly honest, I had absolutely no idea!"

This caused huge amusement and everybody laughed.

Below them in the distance, the ghosts of the Roman soldiers – who had dispersed into a jostling melee of glee – gradually formed back into their ranks and began to march away, back in the direction from which they had come. As they went, they continued to sing loudly what was unmistakably a song of triumph.

At the end of the meadow, they began to fade as a golden, swirling haze started to envelop them. Before long, everything began to blur and become fuzzy. Soon afterwards they had gone completely. Never to return.

# CHAPTER 36

"It was sad in the end, wasn't it?" asked Greesha, struggling to balance on the back of her swaying pony.

"Surely, not for them," replied Father McCafferty, balancing expertly on his horse.

"The feeling of it all being over was sad, I mean."

"The soldiers seemed overjoyed," he replied with a crooked smile that she couldn't see.

"Yes, they were, but there was still something sad about it, in a kind of way."

"Aye, well maybe so, then. In a kind of way, I suppose."

She made a face and shook her head in annoyance as she realised that he had been teasing her. He turned and gave her an apologetic look. There were a few moments of silence, as neither knew what to say, then Greesha became chirpy.

"It is kind of you," she said, happily, "To come with me."

"I couldn't see you go by yourself."

"I don't *have* to have an introduction."

"No, but it would be best if you did."

"That's kind of you."

"You can hardly just rush up to the Laird Grant and say: 'Hello, I need to speak with you about a position in your household', not without him thinking it very strange."

She cast him a look and he shut up. They didn't speak again for a long few minutes.

"Father McCafferty," she said timorously, "There is something I haven't told you."

He gave her a wry smile with one eyebrow arched, "And what might that be?"

"It's two things."

"Pick one."

"We have been on the road for three days," she declared, "And sometimes, at night, you talk in your sleep."

"Oh. Do I? I'm sorry if it disturbs you."

"It doesn't disturb me, but, once or twice – when you have woken and I have asked what it was that you dreamt – you have said that it had been a dream about me."

"I can't control the subject of my dreams."

"No, but, those times, when you've talked in your sleep during a dream about me, you have said a name."

"A name?"

"Yes, Father, but not my name."

"Whose name?"

"The name you say is *Wild Flower*."

"Wild Flower?"

"Yes."

The priest mulled this over for a while before responding.

"How do you know that Wild Flower is somebody's name?"

"By the way that you say it."

"When did I last say that name in my sleep?"

"Last night."

"No!" he snorted, "Impossible!"

"I swear it."

"Last night – and I remember this clearly – it was definitely you that I saw in my dream, Greesha."

She scowled. She was certain of the name he had said, despite his mumbling. It was not, she recalled, anything like Greesha. Father McCafferty waited for her to ask him about the content of his dream, but she didn't. He waited a little longer and then gave up.

"What was the other thing?" he asked, abandoning hope of getting to explain his dream.

"The other thing is something more difficult."

"Does it relate to the Laird Grant by any chance?"

"Yes," she confirmed, then changed her mind, "No."

"Which is it?"

"It's both."

"Both?"

"Yes, Father."

"Surely it has to be one or the other?"

"It's a little strange."

"But it is about the Laird Grant?"

"It is."

"So the answer is yes."

"It's not about *this* Laird Grant."

"There's only *one* Laird Grant, Greesha."

"Yes, but it's not about *this* one."

"How can it not be?" asked the priest, now sounding a little perplexed.

"It's about a Laird Grant in the future."

Father McCafferty brought his horse to a stop so rapidly that its hooves skidded and it struggled to keep its balance. For no explicable reason, Greesha stopped her own mount at the exact same moment.

"In the future you say?" He asked, as if her confirmation were of world importance.

"A long way in the future."

Father McCafferty clapped a hand to his forehead and the slap was so loud it made Greesha jump.

"Of course!" he exclaimed, "Now I understand."

She turned to him, confusion written across her face in underlined capitals. He appeared to ignore her, his eyes unfocused, his head nodding and lips smiling. He was there, but – then again – he wasn't there at all. Suddenly, he shuddered and he saw her again.

"Greesha, do you remember when I first told you that I had seen you in my dreams?"

"Yes, it was in the kind of dreams that are real, because those things genuinely happen."

"I said that I had seen you in the future."

"Yes, you did."

"My dreams, the ones I have been having lately, are about you."

Greesha screwed up her nose.

"It's the truth, lassie. The girl I have been dreaming about, the one who is called *Wild Flower*, it is you."

"She is *me*?"

"Yes."

"But that isn't my name."

"No, but that is the thing that I have just realised. That will be the name they call you, in the future."

"Why?"

The priest tilted his head to the side and gave her a questioning look. In response, Greesha closed her eyes and breathing slowly and deeply, summoned the part of her that dwelt beyond herself. She smiled and gave a chuckle. Then her eyes sprang open.

"It's because they like me!" she exclaimed, "It's an affectionate name."

Father McCafferty looked at her steadily, his gaze unwavering. He continued to do so until she became concerned. Gradually, she began to perceive that there must be something far more significant about, Wild Flower, this other version of her, beyond sharing a name.

"What is it?" she asked, worry creeping into her voice.

"It is not simply that you are her, Greesha. It is that the person you are now, here in the present, becomes who she is, there in the future."

Greesha blinked and looked blank.

"I don't understand."

"Could you imagine what would happen if you projected yourself into the future through a dream and, while you are there, the you that is here could not wake up?"

She felt a moment of panic. Her stomach lurched in her belly. The idea sent a chill down her spine.

"Tell me, Greesha, can somebody reach out and touch you – the you in the future – when you dream of it?"

"Only if I am deeply asleep and only if I am concentrating hard."

"What would happen if you were not, and somebody came behind you and tried to put their hand on your shoulder?"

"Their hand would pass right through me."

"Imagine if you were so profoundly committed to your dream-self in the future that, while you were there, you begin to have dreams of yourself in the here-and-now?"

"What? Can that happen?"

"There are those I know who have done it," he said, gravely.

She paused and looked down at the ground, a captive of her thoughts. Presently, the snuffling of her pony brought her attention back.

"If that happened," she enquired, "What would be the result?"

"I know of one who did it, for sure. They returned years later. I know another who said that they intended to do it and they were never seen again."

Greesha closed her eyes and used her mind to reach out beyond herself. When she spoke, it was with a wariness.

"I feel that the future that beckons me matters very, very much indeed. I feel that I will be drawn deeper and deeper into that time until I find it difficult to drag myself away and back to who and where I am now."

"Does that frighten you?"

"No," she answered immediately, "It should do, but it doesn't."

"Not even a little bit?"

"Not at all. For women, here, in this year seven hundred and ninety-three, are treated badly. In that time to come, in the future, it will be little better than that, except..."

Father McCafferty saw the gleam in her eye and lifted his brows.

"Tell me," he urged.

"Except that there is one particular woman who will refuse to be treated badly just because she is a woman. She will take up a sword against men who disrespect her. She will cut them to pieces. She will make them look like they had never handled a sword before."

She looked at him with the biggest grin he had ever seen, glowing with pride in the mystery woman of whom she spoke.

"She will be glorious! She will be magnificent! She will be superb!"

"A wonderful choice of words for a six year old," Father McCafferty winked.

Greesha laughed and screwed up her face at him.

"I have seen her," Father McCafferty replied, "She is the Queen of the West."

"Yes, she is indeed. She is the very same."

The priest began to look at her curiously, with an odd squint in his eye.

"What is it?" she asked.

"There is more to it than that, isn't there?"

"Yes, but – with what you have just told me – it makes it seem, somehow, absurd."

"Tell me, anyway," he smiled, "I have encountered enough absurdity in my life for it to have little effect on me."

"You told me that you were bound to be a priest, again, sometime in one of your future lives."

"I did."

"Well, in the time in the future of which I speak, there is a priest and that priest is you. It is you as you will be, one day. It is not you visiting that time, from now, in your dreams. It is actually you."

"I am grateful for the confirmation," he replied, "From very early on, when these gifts first revealed themselves to me, I somehow knew it, deep inside me."

Greesha abruptly slapped a hand to her mouth.

"What?" he asked, looking worried.

"When you travel to the future in your dreams – seeing what happens there and being a part of it – what if, you catch sight of your own self? Would that not plunge you into some other world of utter darkness?"

"I have done this longer than you, little girl, but you have done it better."

"I have? How can that be?"

"Your gift for it is greater than mine."

"I have done it for only a short while and I have no proper idea of how it works. I possess no real knowledge or experience of what can and cannot happen."

"You asked me if seeing yourself in the future puts you in peril."

"Yes," she confirmed, "What is the answer?"

"The answer is in what you see when you see yourself. If a person were to see themselves in the future, in the form of a traveller from the past, they would be unable to make themselves out. They would be a blur. All parts of them, from head to toe, would be muddled and foggy. It would be the same for anyone they saw in the future who came from their own time."

"So, Father, me seeing you as a priest, in the future, means…"

She faltered, uncertain of how to express what she wanted to say.

"It means, Greesha, that who you are seeing is not me projected from the past."

She paused and thought about it long and hard. Her expression slowly migrated from confusion to calculation and, finally, to inspiration.

"When you saw me in the future, Father, you knew it was me. You recognised me. You said that my name, then, is Wild Flower. When you saw me, I wasn't hazy and blurred?"

"No, you were crystal clear."

"I was crystal clear," she murmured, thoughtfully.

"What do you think that means, lassie?"

"That means that it isn't just me visiting that time. It is a me who belongs there."

"How is that possible, do you think?"

"Is it that my soul has returned to this world in a future life."

"No, not in your case, Greesha."

"Then how?"

"Think about it."

She frowned, wrinkled her nose, knotted her brow and, before long, closed her eyes for inspiration.

"No! Stop, Greesha. Open your eyes. Don't look beyond yourself. Look for the answer in your head."

Obediently, she opened her eyes and concentrated as hard as she could.

"If I am here," she muttered, "And I only *appear* to be there, then it is the me, here, who has ventured there. If, however, I am *genuinely* there, for real, it is not the me, here, who is there. It can only mean that…" She gave an involuntary yelp and gripped her head in her hands.

"Tell me what it means, Greesha."

"It can only mean that I am no longer here!" she gasped.

"Exactly so!" he confirmed, "Exactly so!"

She was absolutely stunned.

# CHAPTER 37

"Will you cut off his head?" smirked Balgair, gesturing towards the bruised and bloody corpse of Sachairi's uncle, sprawled in a disorderly heap on the ground.

"Maybe I will," he chuckled.

"Nothing could be too grim or gruesome for him not to deserve it."

"My uncle deserves to be hung from a tree by his ankles."

"For the crows to feast on him?"

"Aye, I favour the crows over the worms. The worms are too slow and patient."

They both laughed.

"Maybe, before I hoist him, I could beat him with a club for a while?"

"Take your time. Shall I give you about an hour, or will that not be long enough?"

"I suppose I could just about do him justice in an hour."

They laughed, again.

"Where is the wee lass?" asked Sachairi.

"I don't know," Balgair replied, shrugging his shoulders, "She vanished."

His friend nodded, mistaking his words for an offhand remark rather than the simple truth.

"Do you remember what happened?" Balgair enquired.

"One moment, my guts had turned to water. The next, it was as if I had never feared my uncle for a day in my life."

"I think you took him by surprise!"

They laughed hard enough to grip their sides for relief.

By the time they had recovered their composure, the troops they had left back down the track had caught up and were eyeing the dead body with unrestrained curiosity. The forward scouts had resumed horseback and were biding their time a little way ahead.

Despite being an officer, Sachairi went and pulled the arrows from his uncle's dead body so that he could return them to their owners. Each of the scouts expressed their thanks and returned their arrows to their quivers. In return, Sachairi thanked them for their intervention, for the accuracy of their shots and for saving him the trouble of killing his uncle. It might, he explained, be an easier thing to convey to his father.

Balgair and Sachairi mounted up.

"Perhaps I should drag my uncle behind my horse? It might impress the Queen of the West with my manly prowess."

"Sweep that idea from your mind. I guarantee she would not appreciate it."

"Why? Is she a wilting and wavering lassie?"

Balgair cast him a sneer and clicked his tongue to move his horse forward.

"Sachairi, tell me: What do you know of her?"

"Very little."

"I suppose I know hardly much more, myself, but I know something that you should bear at the front of your mind at all times."

"What is that?"

"It is that The MacDonald holds her in the highest possible esteem."

Balgair caught a glimpse of the frown on his friend's face and noticed his sideways glance.

"The MacDonald," Balgair continued, "Has extremely high regard for her. He is convinced of her worth, her merit and her importance to Scotland."

"So, she is *not* a wilting and wavering lassie, then?"

"As far from it as you could imagine."

"Very well, I'll watch my mouth, then."

"As has been explained to you, we are to go to her with the twelve riders who will be her Honour Guard, and with our thirty other cavalry riders, too. We are to take the fifty troops who are our own and the sizeable army that will be following us, half a day behind."

Sachairi cast him a measured, careful look.

"I hear you," he said.

"I'll have you know that she is formidable with a sword."

"She is formidable?"

"Formidable and fearsome."

"You say this truly?"

"I do."

Sachairi nodded, slowly, contemplating the proposition that a woman could ever be formidable and fearsome with any kind of weapon.

"Surely, Sachairi, you have heard at least one or two of the rumours circulating in these parts, about her fighting skills?"

"I have heard them, but I dismissed them as being nothing more than myths and fantasies invented to give little girls foolish hopes and dreams."

"If I'd had a sister," Balgair replied, annoyed, "I would have made absolutely certain that she had hopes and dreams."

"You are taking this mission very seriously, Balgair."

Balgair brought his horse to a halt, causing everyone to stop.

At first, Sachairi did not turn to face him but, after feeling the other's eyes drilling into him for a little while, he reluctantly met the steely gaze that awaited him.

"Listen, Sachairi, I am Captain and you are my Lieutenant. What we think and how we feel is as important as how we act. We must lead and inspire. Lead by our example and inspire by our beliefs."

Sachairi McRory wanted to be annoyed with the little girl – the one he couldn't actually see anywhere near him – when she tutted her disapproval, mockingly, in his ear. His annoyance, however, simply could not be summoned. He understood that he had crossed a line and resolved to take both her and his captain's reprimand with humility.

"Sachairi, if this mission, your sworn oath to The MacDonald and an absolute loyalty to the Queen of the West are not the most important things in your life, right at this moment, then I suggest you take yourself back home."

Sachairi did not hesitate, for as the invisible little girl kissed his cheek, a wave of new resolve had drenched him like a downpour from a sudden storm.

"You are like a brother to me, Balgair. Whatever is important to you is important to me. If this is how you feel about this mission, then I can guarantee you that I will embrace it with the very same commitment. I give you my word."

"It is good to hear."

"If I, too, had a sister, Balgair, I would want her to worship the Queen of the West with all her might!"

Balgair extended his hand and it was taken eagerly and shaken firmly.

"These twelve men," Balgair declared, "The ones who will be her Honour Guard, they were personally selected by The MacDonald and his Master-of-Arms. You, however, were not chosen by them. You were chosen by me."

"I thank you for that. I will not let you down."

"I do not doubt it for a moment."

Sachairi steered his horse around to face the rest of the Honour Guard, who were sat talking in lowered voices a little distance away.

"Tell me Balgair," he asked, "Is it our hearts, our minds or our souls that trouble us the most in life?"

"In what way?"

"I have always believed in this mission. I have always believed in The MacDonald. I have always believed in the Queen of the West. I have always believed, but never so starkly or so boldly or so absolutely as, all of a sudden, I do now."

Balgair tilted his head, signalling that he would hear more.

"Now that I have been enlightened, I am just like a man who is gripped fervently by a new religion. Such a man wishes all those around him to convert to his faith. I look to the rest of the men who will be our cavalry, and I am overcome by an overwhelming need for them to be as resolute in their faithfulness to her as you and I."

"All forty-two of our riders are, of course, like us, members of the Clan McRory. Would you doubt them?"

"Not the twelve who were elevated, no, but the thirty in our remaining cavalry might not have quite the same respect for women or reverence and dedication to their queen as us."

"You would think that they never had mothers, then?"

"You and I both had mothers who, at one time or other, faced great struggles in their lives. I can only think that, to be a woman, takes a different kind of fearlessness and bravery than to be a man."

"Well said, Sachairi. Think only of the act of birthing a child, if you want bravery."

"By the gods, yes! That must be like having steel spikes driven through your manhood."

"Yes, without a doubt, but could you imagine – having experienced it and knowing how it feels – to willingly endure it for a second or third time?"

"No! Never! I am only too happy to leave the bravery of childbirth to women!"

Balgair swung down from his horse and raised a hand for his Lieutenant to remain where he was.

"Stay here. I will speak to our men. I will be frank and open. I will leave them in no doubt."

Balgair started to walk towards the other ten riders who had been appointed to the queen's Honour Guard. As he did so, they fell silent and paid him rapt attention.

"I have business with the rest of our horsemen," he told them, quietly, "We go to guard a queen and that is a burden that must rest only on hearts that are truly worthy of the privilege. Wait for me exactly where you are. Do nothing unless I command you. When I move away from you, behave as if I have said no more to you than bidding you a good day."

Balgair McRory knew how to move an army safely. Those on horseback all rode in groups, a distance apart. The carts transporting foot soldiers and equipment also travelled with a good space between them. Any attackers would have no opportunity to ambush his entire convoy all at once. Their foes would have to employ a huge force to engage their entire line from front to rear.

Reaching the first rank of main cavalry riders, he motioned in the air for the two other groups that followed them to join up. Soon, there were ten rows of them, riding three abreast. For an hour's ride ahead or behind them, there was no wider section of track nor broader and flatter verges where this could be done.

Balgair motioned, again, and the column arranged itself to allow him maximum visibility of them. The riders from the middle rank to the rearmost rank moved left to form a curve that took them towards and onto the lefthand verge. The riders from just ahead of the middle rank to the frontmost rank moved in the same manner but in the opposite direction.

Balgair unhooked his sword, still in its scabbard, and held it up over his head.

"I know all of you," he shouted, "I have known you and ridden with you since I joined the cavalry. I have trained alongside you. I have fought alongside you. I have endured losses alongside you. I have celebrated victory alongside you."

There were nods and grunts of general approval.

"We are on our way to deliver a promise made by the Laird MacDonald. In doing so, we are all – each and every one of us – his direct representative. Our every action will reflect on him. The way we carry ourselves, the way we conduct ourselves, the way we speak and every aspect of how we behave."

They all sat a little taller in their saddles.

"The Scotland above the Clyde and the Forth is the true, ancient Scotland. It is the Scotland of old," he declared, his words attracting a momentary flurry of cheers, "It is the Scotland that remains loyal to the ways that were handed down to us. It is the Scotland that is fiercely loyal to the bloodline of the old Highland royalty. A bloodline with its roots in the times of the Picts, the Scotti and earliest tribes of the Celts."

Balgair drew his blade from its sheath and held it aloft.

"The swords of the Clan MacDonald, for eight hundred years, have been sworn to the Queens of the West, all the way back to the first of that line: Kiffan the Defiant. It is Annis, Queen of the West, who wears that crown, today. The MacDonald, our Chieftain, swore his sword to her mother, Queen Cydara, who was so treacherously murdered by the very people who had taken an oath to protect her. His loyalty to Queen Annis, the new Queen of the West, is total, absolute and bound by bands of iron."

The sense of anticipation that had been spreading through the men now translated itself into a vague unease.

"The MacDonald honours and bends his knee to a woman. He takes orders and instructions from a woman. He lowers his eyes and salutes a woman. He respects, admires and is obedient to a woman. At the coronation of Queen Annis he laid himself on the ground before her, prostrated on his belly, to show her authority over him."

The tension in the gathered riders was palpable.

"She is the rightful sovereign of the Highlands. She is Queen of the West. She is not some simpering, weak, titled lady who totters in a strong wind and who sniffs perfume from a handkerchief pressed to her nose. She is a warrior. She is from a line of warriors. She is skilled and deadly with a sword, with a spear and with an axe. She does not lead her troops from a safe distance. She does not stay out of harm's way while others risk their lives. She leads from the vanguard in the thick of the battle."

There were mutters of approval.

"If any of you regard a woman as incapable of being your equal or as being an inferior sovereign, compared to a king, then you do not belong here and you do not deserve this honour!"

It was as if he had dowsed each of them with a bucket of cold water. Many appeared to be startled by his words. Little did they suspect that he was nowhere near finished.

"It is in the nature of many men to look down on a woman for no other reason than that she is a woman. It is in their nature that they cannot regard any woman as either their equal or their superior. If any of you is such a man but feels that he can dare to remain in this cavalry, then I urge you to come to me, right now, to feel the wrath of my sword!"

His audience was dumbfounded. Nobody spoke. Nobody moved. The silence was overwhelming. Balgair found himself breathing hard. He could hear his pulse booming in his ears like a drum. He gripped his sword so hard that his hand began to tremble.

From well back in the line of men, a horse snorted as its rider prompted it forward. The rider slid from his mount and his feet echoed with a crash as they hit the ground. Balgair peered at the man and recognised him as Angus McRory.

Angus was a large man, even amongst men who were large. He towered a full head in height above anyone else. His arms bulged with enormous muscles and his chest was as broad as an ox. Balgair felt a pang of dismay. Angus McRory had a brother whom Balgair's father had rescued from a Campbell stronghouse when he had been held captive for ransom. If any man owed his family loyalty, it was this one. Balgair clenched his teeth and pursed his lips into a thin line. He felt a cold fury wash over him.

Angus McRory walked slowly. With each step, twigs and nutshells snapped and crackled beneath his feet. The sound was of a seemingly impossible volume. Shortly, he reached the forwardmost rider of the column. There, he stopped and drew his sword. With great care, he tested the weight and balance of the mighty weapon, tilting it this way and that. Apparently satisfied, he strode on.

Balgair resisted the urge to glance at the other twenty-nine men behind Angus. This huge man commanded both the respect and awe of his peers. Balgair knew that they would all be looking on, spellbound, at the scene that was unfolding.

There were, now, no more than ten paces between them. Balgair, struggling to control his breathing, took a lung full of air to steady himself. Angus appeared totally calm and was not breathing heavily at all.

Carefully, Balgair chose his point of attack on the approaching man, marking out his right collar bone for the initial cut of his sword. He would, he knew, need to swing fast and true and deliver the cutting edge to its target with perfect accuracy to disable him.

There were, now, only five paces remaining between them.

Then, he saw her. It was the little girl he had seen earlier. She was stood underneath some trees, not far away. She shook her head at him and held up both her hands, with her palms facing him, urging him to remain still.

Suddenly, Balgair realised that Angus had slowed. After another step, he stopped. He spun on his heels and held his sword aloft. Balgair decided that this was a distraction and readied himself to strike.

Angus turned to Balgair and met his eyes. Balgair could not believe what he saw. There was no hostility or anger. When he spoke, there was not so much as a hint of malice.

"They need to fear us both," said Angus.

Balgair looked back to the little girl. After closing her palms and lowering her hands, she raised an index finger and held it directly in front of her face, its tip pointing upwards. Like flipping a coin, a golden flame suddenly leapt into the air from her fingertip and tumbled over and over, before gently coming back to rest.

"Hear me!" Angus shouted to the assembled cavalrymen, his voice sending a flock of crows to wing, "Heed my words! Any one of you, from this day forward, who dares to disrespect a woman because you think she is *only a woman* will need to feel my blade, too!"

Ten seconds elapsed, during which even the falling of an acorn to the ground would have sounded like a wooden mallet smacking against the taut skin of a drum. Then, everyone in every direction erupted into cheering and wild applause.

The little girl gave Balgair a smile, a knowing look and a nod of approval. Then, the very next moment, despite his eyes still being upon her, she and the flame vanished into thin air.

# CHAPTER 38

"Where did you go, just then?" asked Father McCafferty, almost accusingly.

"Who? Me?" asked Greesha, her voice a little too innocent.

"Yes. None other," he confirmed, with mock sternness.

"There was a matter that needed my attention."

"Was there, indeed?" he replied, "Well, when you are with the Laird Grant, I hope you will control your urges to lose yourself into a dream while you are awake."

"I will be on my very best behaviour."

"I do sincerely hope so, Greesha."

She frowned at him, becoming a little concerned by his attitude.

"Or should I call you Wild Flower?" he winked, ditching any pretence at being annoyed.

"Perhaps you should!" she laughed.

He clapped his hands in delight.

"Wild Flower," he said, as if testing the name on his tongue, "Wild Flower. Wild Flower. Wild Flower."

"Yes, kind Sir?" she answered, curtseying to him in the manner of an obsequious maid servant, "How may I be of service?"

The priest cackled with amusement.

"You, little girl, can take good care of yourself in the future, for I will miss you."

"I will see you in the future, Father. I will meet you and I will know you in the future."

"Yes, but I will not know you in the future. That will be the me that I will become. It will be my soul, but with another man's mind and body."

"The other man's mind and body will be your mind and body, so the other will be you."

"Yes, but you forget. It will not be me exactly as I am now. That future me will not come about until all of eight hundred years have elapsed. You, on the other hand, will be the future version of you before the sun goes down, today."

She looked worried.

"I will? So soon? You know this?"

"Yes. You know this, too. We cannot wait long."

"Can we not?"

"No, for the Vikings are killing, maiming, slashing and burning the land that will become Scotland, even as we speak."

"But I love you!" she sobbed, throwing herself at him and clinging to him.

Father McCafferty took her in his arms and dabbed her tears with the cuff of his robe.

"I love you, too," he declared.

"And love is immortal," she answered.

Gripping her by the shoulders, he thrust her to arm's length from him. Whilst the movement was abrupt, it was not rough and – left none the worse for it – she was merely confused.

"Wild Flower, precious child, what did you say?"

"I said love is immortal."

Father McCafferty smiled a huge smile and, looking up into the sky, he began to pray aloud.

"I call upon the power that is beyond this world and that was before all worlds. I ask it to bless me with wisdom, insight and inspiration. I ask that it should allow goodness to prevail across this land. I ask for it to command that all evil in this land be vanquished."

"Amen" said Wild Flower, feeling it to be an appropriate response.

"It pains me to imagine what came before time and what realm existed before the stars," he confided.

"I know what you mean, Father, for if I dwell upon such thoughts for too long, my head begins to hurt."

"We are no more significant than a single drop of rain falling into the sum of all the oceans of the world."

"And yet..." she prompted.

"And yet we matter and are of concern to an entity that defies our comprehension."

"An entity that the church attempts to describe and explain within the bounds of our feeble human imagination and vocabulary."

"Spoken like a true six, seven or eight-year-old, Wild Flower!" he guffawed.

They laughed at length. Then, the two fell into an easy silence and she allowed him to engross himself in his thoughts, uninterrupted. There was something, she was sure, that he wanted to tell her and that was weighing on his mind. Suddenly, he clapped his hands and looked delighted.

"Did you receive your inspiration?" she asked.

"Yes! Yes, I did! I feel a certainty about the future that I have not felt before."

She looked at him, sadly, because – she felt certain – their time together was drawing to a close. He saw her look and reached out to rest his hand on her arm.

"Do not worry, Wild Flower, for all will be well."

"All will be well? Without you?" she asked, her voice breaking, "I have escaped from a cruel and savage man who is my parent and now am to be ripped away from a good, loving, kind man who has been a better parent to me, over these last few days, than my father had ever been in the whole of my life."

"Wild Flower!" he choked, "Do not be upset, for all things are possible!"

With a sweep of his arm he gestured upwards.

"I have just looked into the bright blue sky and I saw the stars," he said, "I saw them clearly. As if it were Midnight. Whenever I willed it, I was able to switch back and forth between seeing the sun and the sky and seeing the pitch black night with the moon and a thousand tiny pin pricks of light."

"If you take my hand, I will see it, too," she said, somehow knowing it to be so.

The priest reached and took her hand in his own. In an instant, she was able to see exactly what he had seen.

"You, Wild Flower, have a journey to make. A miraculous journey. You wish to meet the Laird Grant, for you are drawn to do so, and you shall. I will not be able to introduce you to this particular Laird Grant, however, for he has not yet been born."

She hung on his every word.

"When I tell you, you will walk across this meadow, here and now, in the year 793, and you will arrive at the hedge at its far side in the year 1622. All you have to do is wish it to be so with all of your heart and it *will* be."

"And I will leave you – this you who is truly you – behind?"

"No. Truly no. For, as I said: *all things are possible*. Tomorrow, when I wake up, I will come to see you and you will be here. You will have returned from the future. For you, several weeks will have passed between now and then, but for me, it will be just one single night."

She looked at him through blurred vision, her welling tears stinging her eyes.

"You say this truly?" she asked.

"I do."

"Then I will go."

"You told me that when you dream yourself to another place and you feel attached to that place and happy being there, you find it hard to drag yourself away. You said that you feared what would happen if you could not find your way back."

"Yes, I did."

"Well, you will go to the Laird Grant, just as you know you must, and there, in that time eight hundred years ahead, you will do all the things you must do, and then…"

"And then?"

"And then – I guarantee you upon my word – you will find your way back. I know it to be so because I had the kind of dream that comes true and it was a dream about tomorrow. In that dream you were back here with me."

"You say this truly?" she begged, her heart almost breaking and with tears now streaming down her face.

"I say this truly," he assured her, placing his hand over his heart.

Wild Flower took a deep breath, drew herself to her full, but still diminutive, height and kissed Father McCafferty on both cheeks. She set off and, without turning back, she walked across the meadow, willing for the future that she must embrace to come and take her.

The priest watched her, feeling both elated and heartbroken at the same time. He gripped his lips between his teeth, in a grim parody of a smile, to stop them from trembling.

Half way across the meadow she began to shimmer and blur like the heat haze that rises from a stone slab on a fierce summer day. As she moved, she became more and more indistinct, until he could see only a vague outline of her. Within a few moments more, she had completely disappeared, as if she had been absorbed into the air itself.

# CHAPTER 39

"Good heavens!" exclaimed the man, "Where did you come from little girl?"

"I'm sorry if I startled you," replied Greesha.

The man looked around in every direction. He had clearly been startled.

"Well, you certainly took me unawares!" laughed the Laird Grant, his manner kindly.

"I wasn't trying to creep up on you, Your Lairdship," she apologised.

"Your Lairdship? You know me?" he asked in surprise.

"Yes, I do," she replied, then quickly changed her mind, "No, I don't."

"Which is it?"

"It's both. Or, rather, a little of each."

"I'm intrigued!" he laughed.

"If I were to explain, I'm afraid it would be a long story."

"Well, I have the time," he assured her, gesturing to a large rug spread across the ground.

The Laird Grant beckoned to a group of servants who were stood nearby and they hurried across and began to lay out a picnic with cakes, scones, jam and cream.

"I have a guest," he told them, "So lay places for two."

The servants set about doing as instructed and when they had finished, the Laird Grant sat down on a cushion and motioned for Greesha to do the same. She took her place and accepted a plate and some fine cotton towels, all the while trying to untangle her hair which had abruptly become unruly as she had stepped out of the past.

"Tell me, little girl," he asked, "What is your name?"

"I am Greesha, Your Lairdship."

"Greesha?" he mused, pulling a face, "That, to my ear, is a harsh sounding name for such a pretty girl."

"You are very kind, Sir."

"*Greesha*," he repeated, obviously not enjoying its sound.

"You can call me anything you wish, Your Lairdship, and I would be only too happy to answer to it."

"Are you sure?"

"I am perfectly sure."

"Well, you are as pretty as a flower," he said, then laughed, pointing to her messy hair, "But you are a Wild Flower!"

Wild Flower gave him a beautiful smile.

"Well, Wild Flower," he said, trying out the name, "This meadow is my favourite place for a meal out of doors. It has a strange sentimental attraction to me."

"How so?"

"There is a legend attached to this field in my family."

"There is? That sounds wonderful."

"The story has been handed down from one generation to the next, for the last eight hundred years. Would you like to hear about it?"

"I would. Very much."

"Back in the year 793, or so my ancestors would have it, the Laird of Clan Grant of that time, told an unlikely tale that he swore to be the absolute truth. He said that he had sat down upon the hill that rises just behind you, when he saw a priest in his cassock and a little girl arrive and sit down on the grass bank by the road below him."

Wild Flower looked at the Laird Grant, enquiringly, and he leaned forward to speak more quietly.

"To make the story brief, my ancestor said that the little girl stood up, walked slowly away from the priest and then, halfway across this field, she disappeared."

Wild Flower raised her eyebrows.

"My ancestor said that it happened while he was watching her and that he had not looked away even for a second. He said that one moment she was there, then the next moment, she had faded into nothing and was gone."

"Well, Your Lairdship, if he were a Laird and he swore it to be true, then I'm sure it must have happened."

The Laird Grant laughed loudly at this and slapped his thigh at a sudden inspiration.

"Tell me, little girl? It wasn't you, was it? Disappearing into the air like that? Because, just now, it was almost as if you had appeared out of it!"

The Laird Grant laughed, again, finding much amusement in the proposition.

"Me?" Wild Flower chuckled, giving him a beaming smile, "Now that really *would* make a good story, wouldn't it?"

THE END